WILD MALICE

TYSON WILD BOOK FORTY NINE

TRIPP ELLIS

TRIPP ELLIS

1

JD put a heavy fist against the door and shouted one of his favorite phrases. "Coconut County! We have a warrant."

Faulkner and Erickson readied the battering ram.

Mendoza and Robinson covered the rear of the first-floor apartment in *Jamaica Village*.

I hated to do this on a holiday, but the fugitive was wanted for murder. Isaiah Turner had gunned down Curtis King in cold blood on a street corner.

The battering ram smashed the door, splintering the jam. It swung wide. Shrieks and gasps emanated from the apartment.

JD led the way as we stormed down the entrance foyer.

Two shots rang out from the rear of the apartment. There was a brief exchange of gunfire at the back door.

We advanced to the living room, greeted by wide eyes and stunned faces. Lights on the Christmas tree flickered, and shredded wrapping paper littered the floor as children dug into their presents.

The smell of Christmas turkey wafted through the air, along with the scent of various casseroles.

By the time we cleared the living room and approached the back door, the gunfight was over. A breeze blew through the open door, and traces of gunpowder lingered in the air.

Isaiah's family members shouted obscenities at us.

Erickson and Faulkner stayed in the living room and kept a cautious watch on the hallway that led to the bedrooms.

When I reached the back door, I saw the bad news—both Robinson and Mendoza writhed on the ground, groaning.

Isaiah had shot them both during his escape.

Mendoza pointed across the grounds. With a tight chest, he choked, "Get that son-of-a-bitch!"

Isaiah had reached the end of the complex and turned the corner.

We had all worn bulletproof vests. It saved the deputies' lives. Still, taking a direct hit to the chest is like getting kicked by a donkey. It will knock you to your ass and suck the wind out of your lungs. You'll feel like you're dying.

I knelt down beside Mendoza while JD attended to Robinson.

Mendoza's face wrinkled with frustration and pain. "I'm fine. Go get the bastard."

The bullet was embedded in layers of Kevlar. It hadn't penetrated the skin or the back of the vest.

I took off after Isaiah, sprinting across the grounds.

JD followed.

The deputies would be okay. They probably had some cracked ribs and would be black and blue by the morning if they weren't already.

My legs drove me forward, and my chest heaved for breath. I ran as fast as I could through the drab pastel yellow brick complex.

The array of three units looked like army barracks. They weren't much of a step up, if at all. Weeds had overgrown the sidewalks, and there were a few brown patches of grass. Withered palms that dotted the property had seen better days.

I rounded the corner and ran along the sidewalk along Acara Street, chasing after Isaiah.

He'd already demonstrated that he wasn't concerned with taking a life, and he had no qualms about shooting police officers. The kid knew if he got caught, he was going away for a long time.

Isaiah cut across Acara Street and darted left on Oscar.

I followed, rounding the corner with caution.

Crimson splattered the sidewalk.

Isaiah had been hit.

He ran past parked cars and picket fences through a residential neighborhood. The perp angled his weapon over his shoulder and popped off two haphazard shots at me.

Bullets snapped through the air.

I crouched and took cover behind a parked car.

Isaiah kept running.

His white shirt blossomed red. Isaiah wasn't going to get far.

He darted into the intersection at Scrub Jay.

Tires squealed and horns honked.

Bumpers ate the pavement as cross traffic tried to avoid a collision.

A car screeched to a halt.

Isaiah jumped onto the hood to avoid having his knees taken out. The sheet metal dented with a clunk, and the perp rolled off, leaving his impression behind.

He aimed his pistol at the driver and yanked open the door. "Get out of the fucking car!"

The older woman behind the wheel fumbled with her seatbelt.

Then she came up with a pistol that was holstered between the seat and the center console.

She wasn't fast enough on the draw.

Muzzle flash flickered from Isaiah's barrel as he squeezed the trigger twice. The clatter of gunfire echoed down the street. Bullets peppered her chest, and her body twitched. The woman's blood splattered the windshield and seats.

Isaiah yanked her from the car, and her body tumbled to the hot asphalt.

I sprinted toward the bastard, my blood boiling.

He angled his pistol over the top of the car, fired two more shots at me, then hopped behind the wheel.

I ducked for cover.

Isaiah pulled the door shut, dropped the car into gear, then hammered the gas. The little four-cylinder purred, and the tires barely barked as he launched away from the chaos. He weaved around the traffic and took off.

I reached the woman moaning in the street, blood soaking the concrete.

Onlookers stared with slack jaws.

I knelt down and applied pressure to the wounds. "Hang on. Help is on the way."

Warm blood seeped through my fingers as JD called 911. The woman's heart pulsed as blood flowed. Her skin grew pale.

The distant sounds of sirens warbled.

This was not the way I had anticipated the day going. I hoped the woman could hang on until the EMTs arrived.

2

EMTs arrived and took over. I backed away and let them work their magic, my hands crusted with blood.

A crowd had gathered, and traffic was backed up in both directions. Emergency lighting flashed and flickered. Paris Delaney and her news crew arrived, and the cameraman soaked up the gruesome scene.

My body still vibrated with adrenaline, and that terrible sensation twisted my stomach. I watched the medical personnel attempt to save the woman. Mary Mitchell was in her mid-60s with short auburn hair and brown eyes. She was a mother and a grandmother.

Tango One circled overhead along with a news helicopter.

Sheriff Daniels put out a BOLO on the stolen vehicle, and patrol units all over the island kept a vigilant watch for the perp.

"How are Mendoza and Robinson?" I asked the sheriff.

"They're fine. They were taken to the hospital for evaluation." His jaw tightened. "I want this little punk off the street, and I want him off the street now!"

I told the sheriff I suspected Isaiah had been clipped. "If he doesn't turn up at a hospital soon, he might not turn up at all."

There were people out there that wanted to take a personal hand in Isaiah Turner's demise. Reprisal for the gangland shooting of Curtis King. Getting Isaiah off the street was not only for his own safety, but to keep Curtis's friends from making catastrophic life choices. I knew his best friend, Jace Hill, was out for blood. It was a race against time. Who would find Isaiah first?

The cycle of gang violence was never-ending.

The EMTs managed to stabilize Ms. Mitchell. They loaded her into the back of an ambulance, closed the doors, and pulled away.

The siren chirped.

Blood stained the road.

Traffic resumed, and responders dispersed.

Paris Delaney and her news crew confronted me—the camera lens focusing in, a fluffy boom mic hanging over my head. The ambitious blonde was never far from a breaking story.

"Deputy Wild, can you tell us anything about the assailant?"

"Isaiah Turner is a wanted fugitive. If anyone sees him, please contact the Coconut County Sheriff's Department. Do not try to apprehend him yourself."

JD and I trekked back to the apartment complex. Erickson and Faulkner were long gone.

We hopped into JD's convertible 718 Spyder and drove back to the station to fill out after-action reports in the conference room. We typed away under the pale fluorescent lighting, entering the data on iPads.

Afterward, we headed back to the marina at *Diver Down* and returned to the *Avventura*. We crossed the passerelle to the superyacht and Buddy greeted me excitedly as we entered the salon. I knelt down and petted the little Jack Russell. I think he had sensed there was something wrong when we all rushed out earlier.

The boat was a mess from our holiday feast. We cleaned up the wrapping paper, bussed the dishes, and cleaned the galley.

Jack's daughter Scarlett was in town for the holiday and lent a hand. She had seen the news report. "How far can that guy get?"

I shrugged. "I think he's living on borrowed time. He'll turn up, one way or another."

"You think that woman's gonna make it?"

"It wasn't looking good." I frowned.

The whole thing was tragic all the way around.

After we got the boat back in order, JD poured us a glass of the test batch of the *Wild Fury* whiskey. We sipped the premium liquor on the sky deck, watching the sky turn multiple shades of pink and orange. After the week we'd had in the mountains, 70° seemed like the perfect way to spend the winter holiday.

I was looking forward to a fresh start with the new year. Maybe it would bring less trouble. But that was probably just wishful thinking. This year was certainly going to go out with a bang.

The sheriff called the next morning with more bad news.

3

"I need you two nitwits to talk to Eddie Everhart," Sheriff Daniels said. "Says his sister Evangeline is missing."

"How long has she been gone?"

"Less than 24 hours. She told Eddie she was going out on this guy's submarine, and he hasn't heard from her since."

"Submarine? Is that the guy that was on the news a while back?"

"I would imagine," Daniels replied. "There aren't too many people on this island with a submarine. Get over there and see what you can find out."

"I'm on it."

I pulled myself out of bed, showered, dressed, and stumbled down to the galley. I cracked eggs and sizzled bacon in a pan. JD smelled the coffee and staggered out of his VIP stateroom to join me. I updated him on the situation.

Scarlett joined us for breakfast, and we chowed down on the sky deck as the morning sun glimmered on the water. Gulls hung on the draft, squawking.

"If that's the guy I am thinking of, Paris did a story on him," JD said. "Built a homemade submarine. I don't know about you, but I'd think twice about going underwater in that thing."

After breakfast, we left the *Avventura*, hopped into the 718, and zipped across town to see Eddie. He lived in the *Seascape Manor Apartments* on Olive Street. It was a small, teal two-story complex with a central courtyard and open parking.

We climbed the switchback staircase and banged on the door to apartment #204.

Eddie pulled open the door a moment later and gave us a curious look. I flashed my badge and made introductions.

He was in his late 20s with short brown hair, tousled on top. He had narrow brown eyes, an angular face, and a thin Van Dyke beard.

Eddie gave us a recap of the situation.

"Did she mention any names?" I asked.

"No. She just told me she was going on this guy's submarine."

"Does the name Julian Pierce sound familiar?"

Eddie shrugged.

I had searched the web for the story and found a clip of Paris's interview with Julian Pierce.

"When was the last time you heard from your sister?"

"Yesterday. She was excited about it and called to tell me. She joked, *if I don't come back, call the police.*" He frowned. "Well, she didn't come back."

"And you tried calling her?"

"I've called. Sent texts. I went by her apartment this morning."

"What time was she going on the submarine?"

"It was around noon yesterday when she called. She was on her way to the marina."

"Do you know which marina?"

"She didn't say."

"Have you talked to her friends?"

"I called Noelle. She hasn't seen her either."

"How old is your sister?"

"24."

"She'll probably turn up, but we'll look into it," I said. "Do you have a recent photo?"

He nodded and texted a few images to my phone after I gave him my number.

"Pretty girl," I said, surveying her picture.

Evangeline was a knockout. Powder blue eyes, raven black hair, pouty lips, sculpted cheekbones. The kind of woman that could suck the air out of the room and make you do stupid things.

"How did she meet Mr. Submarine?" I asked.

"She said he was a customer."

"Customer?"

Eddie's mouth tightened. He hesitated a moment, then said, "She dances at Forbidden Fruit. I told her not to get involved with customers."

He didn't like his sister dancing one bit.

"We'll talk to Julian Pierce. The only other guy with a submarine on the island I know about is Jay at the Oceanographic Institute, and I seriously doubt she went for a submarine ride with him. In the meantime, if you hear from Evangeline, let me know."

Eddie nodded. "What if he did something to her out on the water? What if he dumped the body?" His mind raced, and his face reddened as he thought about all the terrible things that could have befallen his sister.

"Let's not go to the bad place just yet. Like I said, most people turn up in a few days. I'm sure there's a logical explanation for her disappearance."

"Like what?"

"Maybe she met a guy and ran off with him. Maybe she ran off with Julian."

"She wouldn't go radio silent like this. Something's not right."

Eddie had worked himself up into a tizzy.

"Try to relax. You're not doing yourself any favors by getting upset."

He took a breath and nodded.

We left the apartment, hustled down the steps, and made our way back to the Porsche. I sent a text to Isabella as we climbed in. She was my handler at Cobra Company, an elite clandestine agency that did contract work for the big boys. Need information? Cobra Company. Need something done off the books? Cobra Company.

They didn't have to play by the rules.

JD cranked up the flat-six. The engine growled, and the stereo blasted '80s rock. He backed out of the space, put it into gear, and we rolled out of the parking lot.

I asked Isabella to track Evangeline's cell phone.

I didn't hear back right away, so I called Denise and had her run background on Julian Pierce. Her fingers tapped the keys. A moment later, she said. "No priors. He's clean."

"What's his address?"

4

We drove through the posh neighborhood of the *Platinum Dunes*. Julian had a nice address. Expensive cars, expertly trimmed hedges, multimillion-dollar McMansions. A lot of silver, white, and black SUVs. Mercedes, BMWs, and Porsches.

Isabella texted: *[That phone went off the grid yesterday at 12:21 PM.]*

I thanked her for the info.

I figured the moment the sub went under, Evangeline would have lost cell service. Julian could have a deployable surface buoy tethered to the vessel to provide comms while submerged. But something like that would probably only be used when necessary.

JD pulled to the curb at 571 Conch Court. We hopped out of the Porsche and strolled the walkway to the porch. Towering palms swayed overhead. A silver Lexus SUV was parked in the circular drive, sparkling in the sunlight. The hedges and yard were trimmed to perfection.

I rang the video doorbell, and a moment later, a woman asked, "Can I help you?"

I flashed my badge to the lens and introduced myself.

"I'm looking for Julian Pierce. Is he home?"

"I don't know where that son-of-a-bitch is. And furthermore, I don't care."

JD and I exchanged a glance. Not exactly the reaction we were expecting.

"Mrs. Pierce?"

"Not for long."

"I see. This is Julian's address, is it not?"

"He moved out. He's living in the *Trident Tower*. Or, at least, he was."

"Have you spoken to him recently?"

"As little as possible. What has he done now?"

"I'm not sure that he's done anything. We'd just like to ask him a few questions."

A hint of glee crept into her voice. "That sounds interesting. I'll be down in a moment."

The speaker crackled as the call disconnected.

A moment later, through the privacy glass, I saw a figure descend the central staircase and move to the door. Gwen Pierce opened it up and surveyed us with curiosity. "You two don't look like cops."

"We get that a lot," I said.

JD was in his typical uniform of a Hawaiian shirt, cargo shorts, and checkered vans. His long blond hair hung past his shoulders.

"You were about to tell me what kind of trouble my soon-to-be ex-husband is in." A diabolical smirk tugged her lips that had been enhanced with filler.

Gwen had short bottle blonde hair that hung above her shoulders. She was in her mid-30s with nice bone structure, blue eyes, and a petite figure. Diamond earrings sparkled, and her wedding ring was missing.

"No trouble yet. We're just investigating the disappearance of a young woman."

She lifted an intrigued eyebrow. "Let me guess, he took her for a ride on his submarine."

"Something like that."

She rolled her eyes. "What happened? Did it sink?"

"We don't know yet."

Her face grew solemn. "Well, I hope no one else was on it when it went down. Don't get me wrong, I wouldn't mind if Julian was at the bottom of the ocean. It would be a fitting end."

"So, you're telling me this is an amicable divorce," I said with more than a hint of sarcasm.

She scoffed. "That's a good one."

"We're going to track down Julian. If you hear from him, would you let me know?" I dug into my pocket and handed her my card.

"I don't expect I will hear from him. We only talk through the lawyers now."

We thanked her for her assistance, then headed over to the *Trident Tower*. It was a luxury high-rise with every conceivable amenity—valet parking, 24-hour concierge, weight room, sauna, spa, laundry service, and an attached marina.

We pulled under the carport, and the valet grabbed JD's door. Jack slipped a wad of cash in the kid's palm and told him to keep it up front. We'd been there enough times. They knew us by now.

At the glass entry doors, I waved at the blonde concierge. She buzzed us in and greeted us with a warm smile. "Who's in trouble today?"

"Nobody, yet. Just routine questions. Looking for Julian Pierce."

"1701," she said. "But he's not there. I think he's at the marina. That's where he spends most of his time."

She told us where we could find the sub. I thanked her, and we left the lobby and headed to the dock. There were luxury yachts, bluewater sailboats, sportfishing boats, and a few center consoles.

Jack got a call. He pulled out his phone and grinned at the caller ID. He swiped the screen. "You got good news for me?"

An indiscernible voice crackled through.

JD responded, "Awesome. Keep me posted."

He ended the call.

"Who was that?" I asked.

A sly grin tugged his lips. "Just a little surprise I've got coming."

We found the black submarine. It stood out like a sore thumb. The conning tower and top deck protruded from the water line. It looked like a smaller version of a military submarine with the exception of glass portholes in the conning tower and a few portholes below the water line.

We crossed the gangway and stepped to the deck. The tower hatch was open. I banged on the hull and shouted inside, "Julian!"

He appeared a moment later below. The Florida sun squinted his eyes as he looked up at us. "Can I help you?"

I displayed my shiny gold badge. "Need to ask you a few questions about Evangeline Everhart."

5

Julian was in his early 40s with sandy-blond hair that was a little shaggy. He had ruggedly handsome features, narrow blue eyes, a square jaw, and a dimpled chin. He had the requisite amount of lines, and he carried himself with a slight arrogance. He looked like the kind of guy that would lead a battalion into battle but somehow end up at the rear.

"It's my understanding that Evangeline was a guest in your submersible," I said.

His forehead wrinkled. "Yes, she was a guest aboard. Is there some kind of problem?"

"The problem is her brother can't get hold of her."

He looked baffled.

"Can you tell me what happened yesterday?"

His voice echoed through the sub. "She came over. We went out for a little cruise, then returned. That was it. I tried to call her today, but she hasn't returned my call. You're saying she's missing? I hope she's okay."

"So, you returned to port safe and sound?" I asked with a healthy dose of skepticism.

He picked up on my tone. "Yes. Are you insinuating otherwise?"

"It seems that no one has seen her since your cruise. Where did you go?"

"I took her out, and we submerged near one of the wrecks."

"No incidents? No accidents?"

"No," he said, growing annoyed.

"Did she say where she was going after she left your company?"

"I believe she had to work."

"What's the nature of your relationship?"

His face twisted. "I don't see what business that is of yours."

I ignored his objection. "I understand you are a customer of hers at *Forbidden Fruit*. Did the relationship extend beyond that?"

His jaw remained tense. "I'm not sure what you're getting at."

I shrugged innocently. "Just trying to get a picture of the situation."

"There is no situation."

"I would call a missing person a situation."

"How do we know she's missing? Did she not show up at work yesterday?"

"I don't know. But I intend to find out."

"Maybe you should do that before you accuse me of wrongdoing."

"No one is accusing you of anything, Mr. Pierce. Just trying to piece the puzzle together." I took a breath. "You mind if we look around?"

"I guess I really can't say no, can I?"

I smiled. "Not really. We are entitled to do routine compliance inspections."

"Everything is in order, I can assure you. But be my guest. Look around."

We climbed the ladder and entered the submarine. The metal rungs sounded, echoing through the ship with each step. The air had the smell of diesel, metal, and oil. The con was loaded with dials, gauges, wheels, and levers. Pipes, cables, and hoses ran along the hull to different compartments.

"This is an impressive build. You did it all yourself?"

Julian nodded. "With the help of a few friends."

JD and I surveyed the tube from bow to stern.

"I'm not exactly sure what you're looking for," Julian said. "I assure you, she's not here."

I was looking for blood spatter or signs of a struggle.

The sub was equipped with a head, a small galley, storage compartments for supplies, and four tiny berths. Twin diesel engines powered the vessel on the surface and recharged the dual electric motors. There was a large battery array, and Julian told us, "There are photovoltaic cells built into the top deck of the hull and conning tower that provide additional power when cruising at the surface."

There were two helm stations, one at the bow near the main view portal, and another at the conning tower for surface cruising.

"Why did you build the sub?" I asked.

"To see if I could. Sometimes you have to follow your passion."

I couldn't disagree—unless you were a serial killer, then following your passions might lead to bad things.

The vessel looked well built. Julian had experience in the field and knew what he was doing. I'm not sure if I would want to take this thing to test depth or cross the ocean in it, but it seemed seaworthy.

We searched the cramped quarters but didn't find anything out of the ordinary.

"Satisfied?" Julian asked.

"There's only so much you can see with the naked eye," I said. "Mind if I get a forensic team down here and take a closer look?"

Julian's face tightened. "Is that really necessary?"

I smiled. "It would make me feel better about things."

"I find this whole thing ridiculous, but if it's going to make you *feel* better," he said, mocking me. "Then be my guest."

6

_____

Every surface inside the submarine glowed blue when investigators sprayed Luminol. Not just a few little spots. All of it. The entire vessel had been swabbed with bleach, which reacted with the reagent, causing the chemiluminescent glow.

That piqued my suspicion.

Either Julian was meticulously clean, or he had attempted to destroy evidence. If there was evidence, the attempt was successful.

He had a smug grin on his face, and I began not to like the guy.

"Is there anything else, gentlemen?" Julian asked. "Can I get back to my business?"

"Thank you for your cooperation," I said, stifling my annoyance.

We climbed the ladder, returning to the world of sunshine and fresh air. It took a special breed of person to do an extended tour on a military submarine. A few hours was one thing. Months on end in close quarters, no contact with the outside world, constantly preparing for nuclear engagement—that takes a special breed indeed. Not everyone could hack it. The close quarters of Julian's sub might be enough for some to freak out after a short time underwater. Nothing like the rigors of a military sub, but claustrophobia is claustrophobia. The mind is a powerful thing.

We stepped to the dock and headed toward the parking lot.

"Think he killed her?" JD muttered.

"Right now, anything is possible."

We crossed paths with two guys. Quizzical looks twisted their faces.

"What's going on?" one of them asked. He had short, dark hair with a widow's peak and a scraggly mustache and goatee.

"Just a routine inspection," I said. "Are you friends with Julian?"

They both nodded.

"You know where he was yesterday?"

Their brows knitted.

"Is something wrong?" Mr. Goatee asked.

"No. We're just trying to put a timeline together."

"A timeline?"

"You know a woman named Evangeline Everhart?"

The two exchanged a glance.

"No. Who are you?"

I displayed my badge.

Their faces stiffened.

"What are your names?" I asked.

"I'm Garrison," Mr. Goatee said. "And this is Kent."

I told him that Evangeline was reported missing and gave them the scoop.

Kent had light brown hair and a day's worth of stubble. "Julian said he was taking a guest out on a cruise. I talked to him that evening. He said everything went fine. No problems with the sub at all."

"Did he say what happened to the girl?"

Kent hesitated for a moment, looked at Garrison, then his eyes flicked back to me. "Well, he said..."

Julian emerged from the hatch and peered over the conning tower. His eyes found his two comrades.

Kent stammered, "I don't know if I should really be saying anything. It's not my place."

"If you have any insight into where Evangeline might be, you need to help us find her. If you're covering for your friend, that's obstruction of justice, aiding and abetting... It's a criminal offense."

Kent swallowed hard. "She's missing?"

"No one can get in touch with her."

"He just said they hooked up on the sub." Kent's uncomfortable eyes flicked between me and Julian, who glared at them. Kent puffed up and owned it, defending his friend. "Good for him. She was hot."

"I thought you said you didn't know her."

Kent swallowed again. "I didn't know her. He texted us pictures."

"Pictures?"

His nervous eyes flicked to Julian again, then back to me.

"What kind of pictures?"

"You know."

"Of the two engaged in a...?"

"Yeah."

"Do you have those pictures?"

"You don't need to show them anything," Garrison interrupted.

"They are private photos," Kent stated.

"Those photos could contain a timestamp and GPS data. It might actually help your friend corroborate his story."

"You think Julian had some kind of involvement in that girl's disappearance?"

"We're just following leads, leaving no stone unturned."

Garrison interrupted, "I've known Julian for a long time. We helped build that sub. You're barking up the wrong tree. He would never do something like that."

"Like what?"

"Make a girl disappear." He nudged his buddy. "Come on. We've said enough."

They brushed past us and moved toward the submarine.

We watched them join Julian. They disappeared down the hatch, and I'm sure there was an involved discussion.

"I bet Jay knows this clown," JD said. "Let's see what he has to say."

We headed across the island to the Oceanographic Institute.

Jay was a quirky character with white hair, a white beard, and a jolly disposition. In his mid-60s, he still had the wonder of a child. He'd been exploring the ocean for his entire adult life and still hadn't solved all of its mysteries yet. He'd helped us out in the past, providing gear and gadgets for some of our sea expeditions.

We found Jay in his workshop. Like a mad scientist, he was always developing some new piece of technology. Remotely operated vehicles with articulated arms. Advanced diving suits capable of unimaginable depths. Wireless undersea drones. He'd even built his own submarine, the Trident II— a playful yellow submarine capable of impressive depths.

We won't discuss the fate of the original Trident.

Along with his toys and gadgets, he'd acquired a new assistant—blonde, early 20s, well put together. She had her hair pulled into a bun and wore large tortoiseshell glasses, giving her a studious look. With an assistant like that, I'd spend a lot of time in the lab too.

7

"What kind of trouble are you getting into?" JD teased.

Jay chuckled. "I'm too old for trouble."

"No such thing."

"What are you working on?" I asked as he hovered over a new creation on his workbench.

"Gentlemen, I would like you to meet ROE-D. The Remote Oil Extraction Device. A revolutionary piece of equipment. Sure, there are other similar designs, but this exceeds current technology in every way. It's truly the best in its class, if I do say so myself."

The boxy yellow ROV had a black frame and a large circular drill bit that looked like a snout. A forward-facing camera made it look like a cyclops.

Jay continued, "Do you know how many oil tankers are at the bottom of the ocean with holds full? The ravages of time and corrosive water weaken the structure, eventually allowing petroleum to leak into the water. It's a catastrophe waiting to happen. The environmental impact is immeasurable. It's not a question of if—it's when. Reefs could be destroyed, miles of coastline covered with black slime, wildlife devastated. As they say, an ounce of prevention is worth a pound of cure. We all know these cleanup efforts cost millions, and the environment is never restored to its original state. ROE-D changes all of that. With a depth rating of over 10,000 feet, this little ROV can access some of the deepest wrecks. Magnets allow the device to securely attach to steel hulls. The drill bit can buzz through and attach a valve and hose without spilling a drop of oil. The oil can be pumped to the surface and hauled away where it can be reprocessed, sparing the environmental calamity. Multiple devices can be used at once to speed up the process. It's easy to operate. Anyone can do it with a brief amount of training. I hope to have these in service by the end of the year. And I designed these to be half the cost of the nearest competitor."

"Sounds like you've outdone yourself this time," JD said.

Jay smiled with pride. "Always be improving. That's my motto." He paused and caught his breath. "So, what can I do for you, gentlemen?"

"Do you know a guy named Julian Pierce?" I asked.

Jay grunted.

"Not a fan?"

He shrugged, then softened a bit. "I mean, I find him arrogant and distasteful, but he could be a nice guy."

"How do you know him?"

"It's a small community. DIY submarine builders tend to find one another. We have a forum dedicated to it on the Oceanographic Institute's website. He's posted there on numerous occasions. Got into a few heated debates. He's not shy about stating his opinions."

"What do you think of the submarine he built?" I asked.

"I suppose it's a fine, seaworthy vessel. I don't really know. I've never had the opportunity to inspect it."

"We just did."

Jay lifted a curious brow.

"It's not as advanced as the Trident II, of course," I assured.

Jay seemed a little relieved. "Of course."

"Do you think he's capable of murder?"

That got another raised eyebrow. "Murder?"

"A young woman that was in his company is missing. She went out on the sub with him. He says she made it back to shore."

"But you're not so sure."

I shrugged.

"I can tell you he has a temper. I've seen him get pretty hot at some of our meetings."

"Meetings?"

"The Oceanographic Institute holds meetings once a month where people can gather, talk about the ocean, technology, and conservation." He sighed. "Hard to say. I think anybody is capable of anything, given the right circumstances."

"Do you know what he plans on doing with that sub?"

"I heard he wants to sail across the Atlantic in it. Sounds like a publicity stunt, but I wouldn't put it past him to try."

My phone buzzed with a call from Eddie. His anxious voice crackled through the speaker. "Did you talk to Julian? What did he say?"

8

"That's bullshit, man!" Eddie exclaimed after I caught him up to speed. "Julian knows what happened to her."

"Right now, we have no evidence of a crime," I said.

"So, he's just going to get away with it?"

"We're going to keep looking for your sister. That's all we can do at the moment."

"I see how it is. Just because he's got money, he gets a pass."

"Nobody's getting a pass. I understand how distressing the situation can be."

"No, you don't."

"We will keep investigating him, but without evidence of a crime, we can't make an arrest."

"Lotta good you guys are," he snarked. "I got half a mind to go over there and beat the truth out of him."

"Eddie, I promise we'll handle this. Do not take matters into your own hands. That's just going to complicate the situation. I will let you know the minute I find any new information. Just promise me you'll sit tight and let us handle this."

He didn't say anything.

"Eddie..."

"Fine. But if she turns up dead, and you can't bust that guy. I'll handle it my way."

He ended the call.

I figured Eddie was just talking tough. But you never know what somebody's capable of when they're under stress.

We thanked Jay and left the Oceanographic Institute.

"I don't know about you, but I think it's happy hour," JD said.

We hopped into the Porsche and headed up to Oyster Avenue, looking for trouble.

We found a place to park and walked the sidewalk as tourists listed up and down the boulevard. The amber sun angled toward the horizon, and the avenue brimmed with activity. The scent of grilled fish, chicken, and beef swirled in the air. The strip would pack up after nightfall, but there was always a decent happy hour crowd.

We decided, in the best interest of the case, that a stop in *Forbidden Fruit* was necessary.

The cashier waved us into the club without a cover. Music pumped, and spotlights slashed the hazy air. Sublime beauties pranced around on stage in tall stilettos, breaking hearts and spurring fantasies. Smooth, toned bodies shimmered under the bright lights, clad in skimpy lace bras and panties. Garter belts and thigh-high stockings. Most all of which would get peeled away at some point in time. It wasn't a totally nude joint. For that, you'd have to go to the *Pussycat Palace*.

The air smelled like whiskey, cheap perfume, and glycol fog.

Jacko, the manager, leaned against the bar, overseeing his empire. He waved as we entered, and we approached the New York transplant. With slick black hair, a gold chain, a black shirt, and a gray sharkskin suit, he looked like he could have been a wise guy in a former life.

He greeted us with a firm handshake and a smile. "Is this good news or bad news?"

"We're not sure yet," I said.

His smile faded.

I caught him up to speed.

"Evangeline didn't come in yesterday evening," he said.

"Are you sure about that?"

"I didn't see her. It's not unusual. These girls work when they want to work. There's no set schedule. That's one of the beauties of this job."

"Did she mention that she had any trips planned?"

"Not to me, but you might want to talk to Blaze. They're pretty close."

Jacko surveyed the floor and spotted the blonde vixen. She was taunting a customer with her all-natural endowments. He was smitten, and who wouldn't be?

"Tell you what," Jacko said. "Why don't you guys find a seat, have a drink, and I'll have Blaze pay you a visit when she finishes up?"

We smiled, shook hands, and made our way across the floor to find a free seat. We sat back and took in the sights and sounds of the club. A waitress found Blaze, whispered in her ear, then came over to our table and took our drink order.

After a few more dances, Blaze put on her clothes, chatted with her client for another song, then sauntered across the club to find us. She slinked into a chair at our table and smiled. "Jacko said you wanted to talk to me."

Jack discreetly flashed his badge.

Her smile faded, and her face tensed.

"We just have a few questions about Evangeline."

"When was the last time you saw her?"

"A couple days ago. She's not in any trouble, is she?"

"She's missing."

"Missing?"

"I'm sure she's fine, but nobody knows her whereabouts," I said. "Did she mention anything to you about going on a submarine?"

9

"You mean Julian's?" Blaze asked.

"You know Julian?"

"Yeah. He's in here a lot."

"What was their relationship like?" I asked.

She shrugged. "Julian's cute. Rich. What's not to like?"

"Was there something more between them?"

"I think Julian wanted there to be."

"What about Evangeline?"

"I don't know. I mean, it happens all the time. Entertainers hook up with their customers. Sometimes it's for a price, and sometimes love blossoms."

"You know if she was planning a sudden trip out of town?"

"Not that I know of. But then again, you never know. She's gone away with guys for the weekend before. There are always rich guys coming here *wanting to take you away*," she mocked. *"Get you out of all of this."* She rolled her eyes. "Most of them just want to bang you."

"Did she go away with guys a lot?"

"If the right guy asked."

I dug into my pocket and gave Blaze my card. "If you see her, let me know."

"I will." She paused, surveying the two of us. "Is there anything else I can do for you boys? Would you like a dance while you're here?"

Jack was more than happy to make a contribution to her college fund. She definitely had a masters in the seductive arts.

A call from DEA Special Agent Kyra Cooper buzzed my phone. She'd been recovering from her recent ordeal.

"I've been meaning to call and check on you," I shouted over the music. "How are you getting along?"

"I'm okay. I'm not back on duty yet. Next week." She paused. "Where are you at?"

"Uh... Investigating a case."

"Oh, you want me to call you back?"

"No. Hang on..."

I stood up and signaled to Jack that I'd be outside. I left the club and stepped onto the sidewalk. It was much easier to hear. "What are you gonna do now that the operation is over?"

She had been undercover trying to bring down a major drug kingpin. It hadn't gone well. She'd been kidnapped, tortured, and trafficked. It was a miracle she had been recovered alive.

"I still plan on taking down Hugo Ortega."

"And how do you plan on doing that?"

"I haven't quite figured that out yet. My SAC is reassigning me. Says I'm too close to it. Since my cover's been blown, it's too risky for me to work the area."

"Oh," I said.

"Yep. I'm getting transferred."

I lifted a surprised brow.

"You know where?"

"The pit of hell."

"There are quite a few hellholes. Could you be more specific?"

"Houston. Have you been to that place in August? It's Satan's armpit."

I chuckled. "Ouch."

"Ouch is right."

"It's a major drug hub. I'm sure you'll be able to make a difference," I said, trying to put an optimistic spin on it.

"More than 50% of the drugs that enter the country come through Houston. It's big time. Lotta cartel and gang activity."

"There will be plenty of kingpins there for you to set your sights on."

"Yeah, but this is personal. I have half a mind to take care of Hugo myself."

I frowned. "Never let the job get personal. Clouds your judgment."

She scoffed. "You're one to talk."

It was hard not to take some cases personally. Especially when people were trying to kill you.

"If it makes you feel any better, we'll keep an eye on Hugo. If he slips up, we'll be there to take him down."

"Oddly enough, that does bring me a little comfort."

It was the closest thing to a compliment I'd heard from her. We hadn't started off on the best of terms when we stepped on her toes during a previous investigation. But she was warming up to us.

"Well, I figure I owe you a drink. We probably ought to take care of that soon."

"We're on Oyster Avenue now if you want to join us."

"I'm in Pineapple Bay. My SAC wants me to stay out of Coconut Key. There's a hit out on me. I'm supposed to be lying low."

"I've never known you to do what you're told," I said.

She chuckled. "No, but I've tempted fate enough for now. But if you find yourself up this way, I know a little hole in the wall where we wouldn't be bothered."

"I believe I can make the trip up for a free drink."

"That's all. Don't get any funny ideas."

"I don't have any funny ideas."

"I wouldn't want you to be disappointed when you strike out."

I laughed.

"How's tomorrow night?" she asked.

"I believe I can make that work."

"I don't want to put you out or anything," she snarked.

"It would be a good excuse to get out of town."

"I'll text you my address. Pick me up at eight. We could grab dinner and a few drinks."

"This is sounding like a date."

She scoffed. "It's not a date. One colleague showing appreciation for another."

"So we're colleagues now?"

"Something like that."

"I'll see you then."

I ended the call and slipped the phone back into my pocket, feeling accomplished. Kyra was a smoldering brunette that could ignite steamy desires with a mere glance. She was tough, driven, and daring.

JD emerged from the den of debauchery with a grin on his face. I told him about Kyra.

"Don't forget, we've got that charter tomorrow," JD said.

"What charter?"

"I told you. I chartered the boat to some filmmakers for the day."

I gave him a curious look.

"They're making some independent movie. I figured it would be fun, a little extra cash, and film sets mean hot young actresses."

I gave him a doubtful look.

"I told you about this."

"I don't remember."

I suspected he didn't tell me.

"Scarlett's flying out in the morning," he said. "She wants to do New Year's in New York. She's meeting friends up there."

"I'm fine with whatever, but I'm not sure we have time to babysit the film crew while we work this case."

"We work nonstop 24/7. I think we can take a day off to chill on the boat and make new industry contacts. What could go wrong?"

10

We were in for a crazy day.

The crew loaded gear onto the boat in the morning. It wasn't much—a few LED lights, stands, some bounce boards, and scrims. This wasn't a high-budget production. The majority went into renting the boat for a day.

With a pink ball cap and oversized sunglasses, Scarlett managed to sneak out without anyone noticing her. We said our goodbyes, and she promised to stay in touch. I told her to stay safe in New York. The city had experienced a recent spike in crime and random assaults. But with the way things were going in Coconut Key, I couldn't say the Big Apple was more dangerous.

JD escorted Scarlett off the boat and took her to the airport.

I met the money guy behind the film, and it didn't take long to figure out what kind of shoot this was. With a guy like Don Jammer producing, it could only be one thing.

Don was in his mid-60s now. His waistline had expanded since his on-camera days. He had slicked-back salt-and-pepper hair, a bushy mustache, and saggy brown eyes. He'd earned the nickname *Jackhammer* back in the '80s. He wore a bowling shirt, unbuttoned most of the way, revealing his hairy chest. A gold chain dangled around his neck. He wore cargo shorts and checkered Vans.

I had to chuckle. He could have been a distant cousin of JD's.

"What's the name of this masterpiece that we are making today?" I asked, trying not to sound too snarky.

"Yacht Bunnies 2, All Access," Don said.

"I see."

"Joey here is a great director. Best in the business. And this set..." Don said, motioning to the surroundings, "Amazing!" He leaned in and whispered. "But no one is looking at the set. Still, we're trying to elevate our craft. Gotta have good production value. Joey considers himself an artiste."

He introduced me to Joey Bangs.

"One of these days, Joey is going to hit the big time," Don said. "I hope he remembers us little people. The people who put him on the map."

"Always," Joey said with a smile.

He was in his mid-30s and had narrow beady blue eyes, long stringing hair that hung to his shoulders, and a Van Dyke beard. Joey Bangs was a pseudonym, and I figured this line of work was a means to an end. A way to get production experience and directing credits, though these kinds of credits didn't really translate to Hollywood.

"I'm directing a legit horror film," Joey said. "It's going to be epic."

He introduced me to the cinematographer, Nick Snow. He was a clean-cut kid with short, curly brown hair. Nick went where the money was. It didn't matter if it was a corporate marketing communications video or adult content.

The sound guy, Mike Allen, was a film major at Vanden University. He was an emo kid with short dark hair, dyed blond on top.

The talent arrived not long after. Tara DeVille strutted across the passerelle to the aft deck of the superyacht like a true movie star. She slid open the salon door and stepped inside, lighting up the space.

Tara was a fresh-faced blonde with piercing blue eyes, full lips and flawless skin. She had classic features and an inno-cent girl-next-door quality about her. She could have been a true movie star. What she was doing in *adult film* was beyond me. Maybe she thought of it as a gateway, but rarely does someone go mainstream after starting in the skin trade.

Tara's boyfriend followed behind her, trailing in her shadow. He had a smooth face, brooding brown eyes, and dyed blue hair. It looked like he could have been in an emo rock band with the sound guy, Mike Allen.

The makeup artist set up her station in the salon. It had good natural light and was probably the most accessible location, no matter what part of the boat filming would take place.

Her makeup kit was loaded with every imaginable shade of foundation, blush, and concealer. She had false eyelashes and glue to apply them. An array of shimmering eyeshadows, gallons of hairspray, buckets of brushes and sponges, and other supplies.

"Where's my dressing room?" Tara asked.

I didn't figure her for the modest type, but it was more about having personal space between takes.

All eyes fell on me.

"I can show you to a below-deck guest stateroom that you can call home for the time being."

Tara smiled, flashing her perfect pearly teeth.

I led her below deck, and her boyfriend followed. I pushed open the hatch and gave a tour. "You've got a private en suite, a queen berth, and a flatscreen TV if you get bored."

"Thank you." She slipped into the compartment with her boyfriend and closed the hatch.

I jogged back upstairs. By that time, Sydney Voss had arrived. She was a classic pinup model with an hourglass figure. Most of it was enhanced. She looked like she'd been around the industry for a little while. A little older than Tara. A little more lip filler and a few more Botox injections. Augmentations to the point where she looked plastic.

Diva is the word that comes to mind.

She stepped inside the salon wearing dark sunglasses, a venti latte dangling from her manicured hands.

I escorted her below deck to a guest stateroom, and that's where the drama began.

11

Tara's muffled voice filtered out of her stateroom as I showed Sydney to hers. The conversation drew her attention. "These staterooms are the same size, right?"

"Yes."

"Hers isn't bigger, is it?"

I stifled an eye roll. "No. They're exactly the same."

"You're sure?"

"I'm positive."

I left her to settle in and returned to the salon. I didn't know what the storyline of the movie was or where on the boat they planned to film, but I figured if any action was going to take place on exterior decks, we probably ought to take the boat out of the marina. The neighbors were used to our crazy antics, but this might be pushing the limits.

I talked to Joey about his *vision*.

"This is a complex character study, tapping into universal themes of love, fear, sadness, and joy. An epic struggle between good and evil. An uplifting story about the capacity of the human spirit to overcome adversity."

I gave him a doubtful look.

"It's about two horny girls who bang a rich dude on a yacht," he said flatly. "Moral of the story—be rich."

JD returned with an eager look on his face, ready to start the day.

I pulled him aside in the salon and hissed, "You failed to mention a few details about this production."

He grinned. "What!? They said they were independent filmmakers."

He knew exactly what kind of production this was.

Don glanced at his watch, growing agitated. "Where the hell is he? How am I supposed to make a movie without one of my leads?"

Summer, the makeup artist, shrugged.

Don dialed a number that went straight to voicemail. "Hey! You get your ass here in the next five minutes, or I'm recasting."

Hollywood productions send a driver to pick up talent and bring them to and from the set. That kind of thing avoids delays. This wasn't that kind of production. Don's eyes glanced around the boat and locked on me. "Hey, you. You want to be in a movie?"

I laughed and shook my head.

"It's easy work, and you get to enjoy the company of two beautiful women," he sang, dangling it like a prize.

"I appreciate the offer."

"What's the matter? You don't measure up? Let's see what you're packing."

"I'm more of a behind-the-scenes guy."

"You can have them from behind. You can have them on top. You can have them any which way you like."

"Sorry."

Don's eyes flicked to JD. "What about you?"

Before Jack could contemplate the question, Don spotted Dick Steele strolling the dock. "Nevermind. You're both fired." Don stepped to the aft deck and shouted at Dick, "You're late. Hurry up!"

Dick jogged to the gangway and hustled onto the boat. He was a buff dude in his late 20s and looked like he belonged on the cover of a trashy romance novel. He had short brown hair with blond highlights, a swarthy tan, and a swashbuckling mustache and goatee. His shirt was unbuttoned, revealing washboard abs carved of stone.

"There are a million guys that would kill for your job," Don said. "You almost got replaced by these two." He pointed at us. "You're late one more time, and I'm casting Johnny Iron from here on out."

"I'm here, aren't I?"

"Get into costume."

Dick mocked him. "Aye-aye, sir."

Don grumbled.

This wasn't the kind of movie that had a script. Nobody was interested in the dialogue or character development.

The director filmed a few establishing shots of the girls boarding the boat. I'm sure there would be some cheesy voiceover explaining what they were doing on the boat in the first place.

Once Joey was satisfied, we disconnected shore power and water and cast off the lines. JD took the helm and navigated us out of the marina. The yacht carved through the teal swells. The sun sparkled the surface, and the wind swept across the bow.

For the first scene, the girls sunned themselves on the foredeck, rubbing glistening oil onto each other's skin while gossiping about the hunky captain. Svelte fingers, shimmering legs, flat stomachs, and buoyant peaks. It wasn't long before string bikini tops unraveled and mounds of flesh bounced free.

They primed each other for the main action.

From the wheelhouse, Dick watched the girls with a lustful gaze.

The production was shot with a DSLR, a few small action cams, a drone, and a cell phone. The quality of consumer cameras was pretty amazing these days.

The girls challenged each other to see who could seduce the captain first. Tara and Sydney might not have gotten along offscreen, but on-screen, they were all giggles and smiles.

We dropped anchor in the middle of nowhere, and the production got down to business. With the cameras rolling, Tara snuck into the wheelhouse, drinking in Dick's form as he pretended to pilot the boat, wearing only board shorts and a captain's hat. His biceps flexed, and his abs rippled.

Tara bit her bottom lip. In a breathy voice, she said, "This is a really *big* boat. Is it *hard* to steer?"

"Very *hard*. Want to give it a try?"

"I don't know. You think I can handle it?"

"Let's find out."

Tara dropped to her knees, unfastened his board shorts, and took control of his helm station.

The director, cinematographer, and sound guy crammed into the space. The makeup artist kept an eye on things, and Tara's boyfriend watched with a tight face as Dick Steele took his girlfriend to pound town.

In a hushed tone, I asked Billy, "Doesn't that bother you?"

"It's just acting," Billy said. "She's not really enjoying it."

Tara looked like she was enjoying it quite a bit. Her breathy moans echoed off the bulkheads. Their bodies were slick with sweat.

"I can tell when she's faking it," Billy assured.

It didn't look like she was faking. I'd seen her acting in the first scene, and she wasn't that good of an actress.

The two went at it, hot and heavy. There was on-screen chemistry between the two. A spark of passion.

Billy had seen enough, and so had we. We returned to the salon while the action continued.

"How come you're not doing the scene with her?" I asked.

Billy's face twisted. "I'm focusing on my career as a rapper. I don't want people to think of me as an adult film star."

It was interesting how you could be a gangster, a convicted felon, a murderer, and have a successful music career. But an adult film star wouldn't be taken seriously.

Billy Diamond put on a good front, but I could tell it got to him. He stepped outside to get some fresh air and smoke a cigarette.

"Performance anxiety," Sydney whispered. "Stage fright. Happens to a lot of guys. He can't perform on camera." There was almost a hint of glee in her voice. "Plus, he's not that big. Doesn't quite measure up."

Tara and the captain crescendoed in a frenzied climax. Moans and screams of ecstasy filled the compartment, echoing into the salon.

"Cut!" the director shouted after filming the money shot.

There were congratulations all around like it was Academy-worthy. "Great work! Great work!"

"Let's move on," Don shouted.

Time is money.

"Looks like I'm up next," Sydney said with a smile.

Mr. Steele recharged his batteries within a matter of minutes and earned his nickname. He was ready to go again, this time slipping and sliding around a sun pad with

Sydney, her tight body glistening with oil under the bright Florida sun.

I figured we would have to disinfect the entire boat when the day was over.

Spoiler alert, this scene ended the same way as the last one did. The director yelled cut, and the producer was ready to move on to the next scene. This time, Mr. Steele would have to satisfy both lovely young ladies on camera with mere moments to recover his form.

"Somebody tell Tara she's up," Don said.

The makeup artist hustled below deck while Dick waited around, wearing a robe.

Summer returned a moment later with a panicked look on her face—her eyes round, her skin pale. "Don, I think we have a problem."

12

Tara lay on the bed, her skin pale, her lips blue, her wide eyes fixed. There was no breath in her lungs.

My stomach twisted.

I rushed to her, cleared her airway, and checked vitals. She didn't have a pulse. "Call 911!"

The bed was a little spongy for chest compressions. We needed a firm, flat surface. JD helped me move Tara to the floor, and I began pumping her chest.

I glanced around the compartment, but the culprit was obvious. The powdery residue on the nightstand was a dead giveaway. There was one line left. Judging by the residue around Tara's nostrils, she'd snorted quite a bit.

The production crew looked on in horror.

Billy hovered near the hatch, his eyes round and brimming. He stammered, "What happened?"

I didn't have time for questions. I continued chest compressions. One, 1000...

Two, 1000...

Three, 1000...

Jack grabbed the Automated External Defibrillator. It was a simple device that walked you through the process step by step. I pried open Tara's robe, exposing her chest, and placed the leads. I backed away, clearing the body, as the device counted down.

Tara twitched and convulsed as the device jolted her, trying to restart her heart.

After several failed attempts, the writing was on the wall.

There was no bringing her back.

"I need everyone to clear out of the compartment," I shouted. "Nobody touch anything."

"That's it?" Billy cried. "You're not going to do anything else?"

"I'm sorry, Billy."

Tears streamed his cheeks. He rushed to Tara and started chest compressions, but he didn't know what he was doing.

I tried to pull him away. "She's gone."

Billy wailed, rivulets of tears flowing. He kept at the chest compressions.

"She's been without oxygen long enough now that she has no brain function."

Billy broke down into sobs, and I pulled him away. JD escorted him up to the salon as he bawled.

I pulled the hatch shut and stood in the companionway. I didn't want anybody disturbing the scene.

The Coast Guard arrived, and EMTs attempted one more time to resuscitate Tara, to no avail.

I found Billy in the salon, sitting on the settee, his head in his hands.

"Where'd she get the coke?" I asked.

He sniffled and wiped his eyes. "I don't know."

"Was that a regular thing for her?"

He hesitated.

"I need answers, Billy."

"I mean, she wasn't an addict or anything."

"Did she have any heart or medical conditions?"

"Not that I know about."

I asked the question in a different way. "Where does she usually get her drugs from?"

"I don't know," he stammered.

I gave him a hard look.

"I swear. I don't know."

"Does anybody know?" I asked the crowd.

There were a lot of looks to the deck, averted eyes, and nervous glances.

"Does anybody else have any illegal narcotics on board?" I shouted.

There were more dumb looks.

"No," they mumbled.

"Alright, nobody is getting off this boat until I've had an opportunity to interview each and every one of you individually."

"What's the big deal?" Sydney asked. "She OD. It happens."

Her callous response drew more than a few glares.

"What's your fucking problem, Sydney?" Billy growled.

"I don't have a problem. It's not my fault some people can't handle their high. She shouldn't have been doing it in the first place."

Anger twisted Billy's face. "Shut up! You're one to talk."

Sydney balked. "I don't do that shit anymore."

"Did anybody talk to Tara or see her after she went back to her stateroom?" I asked.

Summer said, "I knocked on the hatch and said Joey was ready to shoot. She didn't respond, so I opened the door, and there she was."

"Did you touch anything in the room?" I asked.

Summer shook her head.

"I don't understand," Joey said. "You're acting like this was a murder or something."

"It is a homicide. Someone sold her the drugs. I want a name."

I didn't figure I'd get one.

Nobody wanted to rat out their dealer. I suspected whoever sold Tara the coke had sold other people on the crew drugs as well. Cocaine went with the entertainment industry like icing on cake.

We waited for Sheriff Daniels and the medical examiner to arrive. The Defender class patrol boat pulled to the stern and tied off. The sheriff boarded the swim platform with the medical examiner and her team.

Daniels gave me a stern look. "You want to tell me what's going on here?"

A porn star overdosing on a yacht owned by two Coconut County deputy sheriffs wouldn't make for a good headline.

13

I talked to Billy on the aft deck. The rest of the film crew were inside. "It would be really helpful if you could tell me where she acquired the drugs."

His jaw flexed. "I'm telling you. I don't know."

I looked deep into his eyes. "If you think you're protecting somebody—"

"Why would I protect somebody if they're responsible for Tara's death? I loved her, man."

"Were you with her when she was using today?"

"No."

"Was anybody else with her at the time?"

"How should I know?"

"Where were you?"

"I was on the deck smoking a cigarette. We partied pretty hard last night. Tara said she had a headache. She wanted to take a nap between scenes, so I left her alone."

"Was she on anything else? Maybe taking some other medication?"

Billy shook his head.

One by one, we talked to the rest of the cast and crew on the aft deck. Of course, nobody saw anything, and nobody admitted to giving her drugs.

I asked Sydney about their relationship. "I sensed a little tension between you two."

"I'm not gonna say she was my best friend. She's my main competitor. It's a cutthroat business."

"You don't seem too broken up about her death?"

"I'm crying on the inside," she snarked.

I gave her a look.

"What do you want me to say? It sucks. I feel bad for her. Will I get more jobs because of this? Probably."

"Where were you when this happened?"

"I was on the foredeck with Dick. Then I went to freshen up for my next scene. Summer touched up my makeup. I think I went back to my stateroom for a minute. What's with all the questions?"

"Just trying to sort out what happened."

"Isn't it obvious what happened?"

"You didn't give her any drugs?"

She looked at me flatly. "That shit's expensive. I'm not giving it away. Not to people I don't like."

"You seem like a very compassionate individual," I said.

Sydney sighed, and her eyes narrowed. "Newsflash. Girls in this industry OD all the time. You guys are acting like this is the first time this has ever happened. I'll let you in on a little secret. Most of the girls that get into this business can't handle it. It's fast money and a lot of attention. It's based solely on your looks and your willingness to perform. You're the hot fresh face one week, and your yesterday's news the next. This business will chew you up and spit you out, and only afterward will you realize that you've made a choice that will affect you for the rest of your life. It stays with you forever, like a tattoo."

"That doesn't seem to bother you."

"It doesn't. I try to stay detached. I've made my choices with a clear head. I knew what I was getting into, and this life-style has afforded me certain luxuries. But it takes a toll on some girls. They get depressed. They try to self-medicate, which leads to addiction. Then when the industry leaves them behind, they have nothing."

"Maybe you should counsel some of these fresh faces."

"Maybe I should. I've tried, but they don't listen. So, for the most part, I've decided to save my breath."

"What was it about Tara that you didn't like?"

She paused for a moment and took a breath. Her eyes glanced inside the salon. Nobody was paying attention to us at this point. "It's not that I didn't like her. Hell, I barely knew her. We worked together occasionally. I'm a professional, and I do what I'm supposed to do with a smile." She sighed. "If I'm being honest, it's probably jealousy. She's younger, she's gorgeous, and all-natural. I'm doing everything I can just to keep up."

The makeup artist slid open the salon door. "I hate to interrupt, but Sydney, they're ready for you on set."

I lifted a surprised brow. "On set?"

"Well, Don paid for the charter, and he needs to get one more scene in the can. You know. Show business."

Sydney excused herself and shuffled into the salon.

I exchanged a glance with JD.

"Maybe we should stop chartering the boat," I said. "It's not like we need the money."

JD shrugged. "This could have happened to anybody."

Something caught Jack's eye. He squinted at the glimmering water, then pointed. "What the hell is that?"

14

W e grabbed the sheriff and hopped into the patrol boat. I cast off the lines as he cranked up the twin outboards. It became obvious what we were dealing with as we drew closer.

Daniels groaned.

He maneuvered the boat near the bloated corpse, and we carefully fished the body out of the water and pulled the remains onto the deck. Decomposition gasses will bring a corpse to the surface if not properly weighted down. I didn't need the medical examiner to tell me the body had been in the water less than 24 hours. My first thought was that someone had taken matters into their own hands.

Julian Pierce had two gunshot wounds to the chest. Despite the holes, there were enough gasses in his stomach and intestines to make him buoyant.

He was relatively intact. A few creatures had nibbled here and there, but the sharks hadn't gotten to him yet. I wondered how many bodies got dumped and chowed on by the toothy bastards that we never found.

Julian's skin was already starting the slough. The foul smell, mixed with the briny water, hit my nostrils. It wasn't pleasant. Julian had a surprised look on his face. It was probably the last expression he made.

"Why is it always complicated with you two?" Daniels asked, hovering over the body.

We shrugged innocently.

"Things get complicated all on their own," I said.

"Any idea who filled him full of lead?"

"I've got a pretty good guess."

We headed back to the *Avventura*, tied off at the swim platform, and boarded the boat. Brenda greeted us on the aft deck. "I thought you left me here."

"We wouldn't do a thing like that," JD said with a smile.

"We've got another victim for you," the sheriff said.

"I see that."

The sheriff gave her the details.

We escorted her back to the patrol boat. It pitched and rolled on the swells as she snapped on a fresh pair of nitrile gloves and examined the remains.

I glanced back to the *Avventura*. Dick had Sydney bent over the gunwale on the foredeck, plying his craft. It was business as usual.

Daniels shook his head. "I'm going to take a lot of heat on this one because of you two."

I raised my hands innocently. "I didn't have anything to do with it."

His eyes narrowed at me.

"Small caliber," Brenda said. "Probably 9mm."

It wasn't anything we didn't already know.

"Time of death is going to be a little tricky. I need to factor in water temperature, but rough guess... This happened late last night or early this morning."

"How do you think he got out here?" Daniels asked.

"Well, whoever killed him probably dumped him," I snarked.

He gave me a look. "Can we just get a week? A week where nothing happens."

15

Brenda and her crew bagged the remains of the deceased and transferred Tara's body to the sheriff's patrol boat. The Coast Guard went on their way, and Daniels headed back to the station with Brenda and the investigators.

We weighed anchor, and JD took the helm. We cruised back to Coconut Key while Joey Bangs wrapped up his film.

I collected contact information from everyone.

Billy looked like a zombie—all the emotion and life drained from him.

It was a quiet ride back. Nobody had much to say.

At the marina, JD navigated us into the slip. I tied off and reconnected shore power and water.

Don shook my hand. "We appreciate your hospitality. Tragic that we lost a rising star today."

He gave a solemn frown, hung his head for a moment, then moved on, probably never to think of it again.

The cast and crew gathered their things and crossed the passerelle to the dock. I told Billy to get in touch if he had any sudden revelations about where the drugs came from.

I didn't expect to hear from him.

JD and I cleaned up the place, gathered the sheets from the guest staterooms, and swabbed the deck, sun pads, and any other area that needed attention.

I took a hot shower and got cleaned up for my sort of date with Kyra. I needed to wash the day away. I felt dirty, and I wasn't even involved in anything.

Jack tossed me the keys to the Porsche. I guess he was feeling a little guilty about the drama today. None of this would have happened if we didn't charter the boat. But then again, we might never have found Julian Pierce.

"I want it back in one piece," he said.

The last time I wrecked his car, it wasn't my fault.

I said goodbye to Buddy and sent Kyra a text that I was on my way. I hustled down the dock and didn't get far before I was accosted by Paris Delaney and her news crew. The camera framed me up.

"Deputy Wild, can you confirm that both Tara DeVille and Julian Pierce died on your yacht today?"

My face tightened. This felt like an ambush. "You've got your facts wrong. That's all I can say at this time."

I hustled past them, and Paris shouted more questions.

I climbed into the 718 and twisted the ignition. The engine growled with a glorious rumble. The Spyder was a special car. Six cylinders of meticulously crafted perfection.

I backed out of the parking space, put the car into gear, and rolled out of the parking lot.

Paris and crew filmed my departure. I didn't even want to think about how she would characterize this. It was too juicy a story to pass up. And she worshiped on the altar of attention.

When I turned on the road, my foot grew heavy, and the engine howled. With the top down, the wind swirled, and music pumped through the speakers. This was the perfect car for a short road trip.

I tried to clear my head as I cruised up to Pineapple Bay. But the faces of Tara DeVille and Julian Pierce lingered, burned into my retina. In the morning, I figured we'd pay a visit to Eddie Everhart. He was my prime suspect.

Kyra was hiding out in the *Bayview Lodge*. A cozy little B&B on the water, overlooking a marina. The DEA was picking up the tab, and she was registered under an assumed name for an added layer of caution. She had an apartment in Pineapple Bay but was keeping her distance.

I found a place to park on the street, hopped out, and strolled the red brick walkway to the veranda. It was a two-story French colonial ensconced by tall palms and other verdant foliage. I texted Kyra that I was here as I stepped into the foyer.

Nobody was around.

I climbed the central staircase to the second floor and banged on #202.

Footsteps clattered against the hardwoods as Kyra approached the door. The peephole flickered, then she twisted the deadbolt and pulled open the door with a smile. "Right on time."

She looked stunning. Her tight black cocktail dress was like a second skin, displaying her magnificent attributes. The high hemline revealed toned thighs and sculpted calves, accentuated by stiletto heels. Her makeup was flawless, and her smoky eyeshadow shimmered.

"You don't look too bad," I said.

For this not being a date, she sure had dressed the part.

She shifted on one hip and gave me a sassy look. "Is that supposed to be a compliment?"

"Well, the last time I saw you—"

"We're not gonna talk about the last time you saw me."

It was at the hospital, and she was black and blue. The bruising on her cheeks and under her eye had either faded or she'd covered it up with concealer.

She slipped out of the room and locked the door behind her. The faint traces of her perfume swirled, and my heart beat a little faster.

"How was your day?" she asked as I escorted her down the steps.

I responded with a grim chuckle.

"Sounds like there's a story there."

"There is. I'll tell you all about it at dinner. I made reservations at Blue. You know the place?"

She smiled. "I do. A man of action. I like that."

We walked across the street, and I grabbed her door. She slid into the heavily bolstered seat, and I hustled around to climb behind the wheel.

"Nice ride."

"It's Jack's."

"You guys are definitely on the take."

I laughed again, cranked up the engine, and dropped it into gear. I pulled away from the curb and zipped to *Blue*. The valet rushed to grab our doors. I slipped a few bills in his palm and told him to keep it up front. He was happy to do so.

Staff pulled open the entry door, and I escorted Kyra inside. The sumptuous brunette drew plenty of eyes as the hostess seated us in a booth by the window that overlooked the water. *Blue* was a fancy, five-star seafood restaurant with dim ambient lighting and hushed conversations. Smooth piano music filtered through the restaurant. Forks clinked against plates, and the delightful aroma of surf and turf wafted about.

I kept a watchful eye on our surroundings, and so did Kyra. She played it cool, but I think she was a little unnerved, knowing there was a contract out on her life. It was probably a little foolish to be out and about, but Hugo Ortega and his goons would be looking for her in Coconut Key, not in Pineapple Bay.

"The lobster bisque is really good here," she said.

"That's good. I'm a connoisseur of bisque."

We perused the menu housed in an elegant leather folio.

A cute blonde waitress stopped by the table and introduced herself. Cassie read the specials, and we ordered a round of drinks to start.

Cassie darted away, and Kyra said, "So, I have a confession to make."

I lifted a curious brow. "We haven't started drinking yet, and you're already making confessions?"

She shrugged.

"You don't strike me as the confession type."

Kyra laughed.

I waited for her to divulge her secret, but she hesitated.

16

"**S**pill it," I said.

Kyra's eyes stared deep into mine. Her lips parted, the words on the tip of her tongue. Then something caught her eye across the room. In a low groan, she muttered, "Shit!"

She slinked and scooted to the far corner of the booth. "Don't look, but guess who else is dining here tonight?"

I pulled out my phone, launched the camera, and spun it around into selfie mode. I held it on the table so I could see behind me.

Hugo Ortega had returned from the restroom and taken a seat a few tables over. He was having dinner with two other gentlemen. I don't think he'd seen us yet.

Hugo was a ruthless gangster. But he never did the dirty work himself. His nephew Santiago had been denied bail and was still behind bars. He refused to cooperate with the prosecution. Hugo's right-hand man was dead. I had no doubt other thugs had stepped up to fill the vacancies in his organization, but I figured he might be low on manpower. He put an open contract out on the street for Kyra—the first one to take her out would get the prize. But would someone be bold enough to make an attempt in a public place like this?

We contemplated our next move.

Cassie returned with our drinks. "Are you ready to order?"

Kyra and I exchanged a hesitant glance.

"You want to go?" I asked.

"Is there something wrong?" the waitress asked.

"I'm not gonna let him push me into the shadows," Kyra said, mustering her resolve. "I doubt he'll try anything here, anyway." She addressed Cassie. "I think we know what we want. I'll have the lobster bisque to start, followed by the 8-ounce filet, topped with lump crab meat and a side of sautéed mushrooms."

"How would you like that cooked?"

"Medium rare plus."

"And for you, sir?"

"The same."

The waitress collected the menus with a smile. "By the way, the gentleman at that table has picked up your tab." She pointed to Hugo's table.

I cringed, and Kyra peered around me at the thug.

Hugo waved and smiled.

Kyra grit her teeth and forced a smile. "You know what? Put their bill on our tab."

"We'll this is awkward," Cassie said.

"You have no idea," Kyra muttered.

"That's mighty generous of you. I'll see if Mr. Ortega accepts. I should tell you that the wine they are drinking is rather... expensive. It's a Domaine Lémieux Grand Cru."

Kyra didn't flinch. "That's fine."

I almost swallowed my tongue. She had no idea what she was getting into.

Cassie collected our menus and darted away.

I thumbed through the wine list, turned it around, and displayed it to Kyra, pointing at Hugo's selection.

Her eyes rounded when she saw the price. "Well, that's impressive."

17

"I'm beginning to think this wasn't such a good idea," Kyra said.

"So much for lying low," I said dryly.

"At least everything's on the table. I prefer standup fights to all this sneaking around."

"What do you think he's doing in Pineapple Bay?" I asked.

"Establishing new connections. Maintaining old relationships. Who knows?"

The waitress delivered our bisque. It was creamy and smooth. Rich with a hint of sherry and large chunks of fresh lobster.

Hugo and his associates finished their meal and left the restaurant. I suspected he let his people know we were here. I was prepared for anything.

We sipped our whiskey and chit-chatted, both keeping cautious eyes on our surroundings.

The steaks were tender and juicy, cooked to perfection. Butter, lemon pepper, and a hint of rosemary.

Dessert rolled around. I'm partial to Key Lime pie, but the carrot cake was impressive.

I grabbed the bill when it came.

"No way," Kyra protested. "I'm buying."

"I picked the restaurant."

"This was supposed to be me buying you a drink to thank you for all your efforts."

"We didn't really do much."

"It's the thought that counts. Hand it over," she said, extending her palm, waiting for me to relinquish the leather folio.

I opened it and gave a glance at the tab. As I expected, it was astronomical due to Hugo's wine. I pulled out a credit card, slipped it into the folio, and handed it to the waitress as she passed.

Kyra glared at me. "Now I feel like I owe you something."

"You don't owe me anything."

"I almost feel bad. That's an expensive dinner, and you're not going to get any ass out of it."

I chuckled. "Who said I was interested?"

She rolled her eyes. "I've been around long enough to know when a man is interested."

"Well, I'm not that easy. If you think I'm gonna let you sleep with me just because I bought you a fancy dinner, you're sadly mistaken."

Her face crinkled. "Is this some kind of reverse psychology?"

I laughed again. "So, what's this confession you have to make?"

"Changing the subject?"

"Just curious."

"Well, I did have an ulterior motive."

I gave her a look.

"I want you to help me take down Hugo Ortega."

"You are off the case. You're getting transferred."

"I'm not talking about an official capacity."

"We're talking vigilante justice?"

"No. I'm talking about working a case on the side. Building it up and bringing him down."

"All in the next week before you leave town?"

"I realize that may not be possible. But what I'm really asking is for you to stick with this until he's behind bars."

"I told you, I will stay on him."

"I understand. But people say a lot of things. They make promises they don't keep. Life gets in the way, and they move on to other things."

"I keep my promises."

She gave me a long, hard look, her eyes staring deep into mine.

"Look, it's not going to be overnight," I said. "You know that. The guy is slick. He doesn't get directly involved. Somebody's gotta turn on him, and so far, no one's been willing. Not even that scumbag nephew of his."

She sighed. "It just irks me to no end that people like that get to walk around with impunity."

"Live by the sword, die by the sword. Sooner or later, this business catches up with everybody."

"There are plenty who get away with it."

I exhaled. "Sometimes you gotta know when to walk away. Now might be that time for you. Go to Houston. Start a new life. You'll forget all about Hugo Ortega. There are plenty of scumbags there to deal with."

Her face tightened. "I don't know. Maybe you're right. Sometimes I think I need to walk away from this whole thing. Do something else with my life. I mean, what good are we really doing, anyway? We take one guy down, and another one pops up. All we do is create a power vacuum for somebody else to fill."

"It's a failure of policy. But I don't get involved in politics."

"Why do you get involved at all? You don't have to."

"The answer to that question is long and complicated. And wasn't the point of this evening to unwind and uncomplicate things."

A smirk tugged her plump lips. "I suppose."

"So let's find a place to get uncomplicated. You said you had a place in mind."

"I do."

We slid out of the booth and weaved through the restaurant to the exit. My pistol was holstered in my waistband for an appendix carry. I kept a hand at the ready, just in case.

At the hostess stand, I said, "Stay here. I'll have the valet pull the car around, then signal for you."

She nodded.

I moved to the door, glanced around, then stepped outside. I kept my head on a swivel as I handed the ticket to the valet. He had parked the car near the entrance, next to a red Ferrari.

18

The valet hustled to the podium, matched the ticket to the key, and jogged to the car. It wasn't the same guy I had left the car with. The original attendant was trotting through the lot toward another car.

The valet pulled the 718 around.

I wanted to get out of the lot quickly, so I hustled to the driver's side and slipped a wad of cash into the valet's hand.

"Thank you, my friend," he said with a smile.

He ran to the passenger side and pulled open the door, even though he hadn't seen us arrive together. Kyra was still inside.

I noticed gang tattoos poking above his collar.

Alarm bells went off.

Kyra emerged from the restaurant and hustled toward the car.

I sprinted around the vehicle and shouted, "Stay back!"

The valet drew a pistol and took aim at her.

Nearby patrons shrieked.

Kyra's eyes went wide.

I tackled the thug to the ground from behind before he could get a shot off. He crunched against the concrete with a groan, and the weapon clattered away. I grabbed a fistful of his greasy hair and smashed his face into the pavement several times. His nose shattered, spattering the ground with blood. He groaned and struggled, but I wrestled him under control and slapped my cuffs around his wrists.

So much for uncomplicated.

By that time, Kyra was at the car. She scooped the weapon from the concrete and called 911. I kept a knee on the perp's back, pinning him against the ground.

Pineapple Bay was within Coconut County. I had jurisdiction here.

"Who hired you?" I asked the goon.

He didn't say anything.

"Start talking!" I demanded.

He didn't comply. I figured this wasn't his first time in cuffs.

A Pineapple Bay PD unit showed up five minutes later. I yanked the perp from the ground and stuffed him into the back of the squad car. I flashed my badge to the officer and told him I wanted to interrogate the perp.

He seemed agreeable.

His partner took witness statements, then they drove the perp to the local station where he was processed, printed, and put into an interrogation room.

Kyra and I followed.

"You saved my life and bought me dinner," she said, buckling her safety belt. "Not bad for a first date."

"This isn't a date, remember?"

Kyra smirked.

At the station, I tried to have another chat with the scumbag. Kyra and I sat across the table from him in the tiny interrogation room.

"I know Hugo Ortega is behind this. Give me something that will take him down, and I'll talk to the state's attorney. We'll work out some kind of deal for you."

He glared at me with evil eyes. "I want to speak to my attorney."

He knew the game. That was the end of our conversation.

Lorenzo Castro was in the system with priors for assault, possession, and a few other charges. I sent his information to Isabella after we left the tiny room.

"You know, I hate to be a party pooper," Kyra said, still on edge. "But I think I've had enough adventure for one evening."

"That's probably a good idea. We can always grab a drink another time."

"I do have a bottle back in my hotel room," she said, casually throwing it out there.

Sounded reasonable to me.

We left the station, and I made sure we weren't followed back to the bed-and-breakfast. I made erratic turns, doubled back a few times, and took an unusual route. I parked the car, escorted Kyra into the bed-and-breakfast, and up to her room. She slipped the old skeleton key into the slot and twisted the handle. The door creaked open, and we pushed inside.

She flipped the deadbolt behind us right away.

It was a quaint little space with a sitting area. There was a sofa, a TV, and a coffee table. Windows overlooked the marina, and French doors provided access to the terrace. In my estimation, it was a security threat.

The queen-size bed looked sturdy.

"You might want to think about getting out of town sooner rather than later," I cautioned.

"Are you trying to get rid of me?" she asked, moving to the dresser and pouring two glasses of whiskey.

"Just thinking of your safety."

She returned and handed me a glass.

We clinked.

"I appreciate your concern."

Her smoldering blue eyes stared into mine as her lips wrapped around the glass.

Oh, to be that glass.

She inched closer, and I suspected this was about to turn into a real date. I was perfectly fine with that.

My heart thumped with anticipation.

She lifted on her tiptoes, and I pulled her into me as our lips collided. The taste of her lip gloss mixed with the remnants of whiskey as our tongues danced. Her lips were soft and pillowy, and her body warm. The whiskey was good, but I needed to free up my hand for extracurricular activities.

With our lips locked, we shuffled toward the dresser, and we both set our glasses down, then proceeded to maul each other.

This had been building for a long time.

The temperature in the room got hotter.

My hands caressed her thighs and lifted the hemline of her tiny skirt over her hips. I traced the curves of her smooth skin, grabbing pert handfuls.

Soon, her panties were sliding down her creamy thighs. She stepped out of them as they hit the hardwoods, kicked off her high heels, and slipped the straps of the dress from her shoulders.

Desire burned as she shimmied out of the form-fitting fabric.

She was a vision.

Pert, gravity-defying endowments begged for attention.

Her flat stomach was toned, and her legs divine.

She sauntered toward me as I peeled off my shirt.

19

Kyra fumbled with my waistband. Pretty soon, there was nothing between us. We fell onto the bed and tumbled around for a while, rumpling the sheets and putting on a show for the neighbors. I'm sure everyone in the place heard the moans and screams of ecstasy.

Our hips collided, and the chaotic symphony of passion crescendoed. We collapsed beside each other, sweaty and exhausted, heady with a swirl of whiskey and dopamine.

"I'm glad that assassin wasn't successful," I said.

"Me too," she said, stroking my chest with her delicate fingers. She nuzzled close, my arm around her.

"I really think you should exercise more caution going forward."

"Aw, is that concern I detect?"

"It might be."

"If you're that concerned, get him off the street."

She kissed my neck, nibbled on my ear, and had a few naughty suggestions about round two. It wasn't long before she straddled my hips and put on a convincing argument to do it again.

She wouldn't get much debate from me.

We did our best to wear out the mattress, and the headboard rattled the wall.

It was too bad she was leaving town. I could get used to this kind of thing. She was smart, sexy, ballsy, and just crazy enough to keep it interesting.

I spent the night with the vixen curled up beside me. I kept my pistol on the nightstand and never truly let go of consciousness. It was that half-sleep, listening for anything unusual. I was sure no one had followed us, but a part of me kept expecting someone to break down the door and light the place up with molten copper.

I was up by the time the morning sun pierced the windows, painting squares of light on the hardwoods.

We revisited last night's activities just to make sure it was as good as we remembered.

It was.

We took a shower, then headed down for breakfast. There were a few other couples dining, and we got the odd look here and there. Nobody else in the bed-and-breakfast had as much fun as we did.

"Maybe you should switch locations," I suggested when we returned to the room.

"I like it here. I think it's safe. But I'm not going out anymore. And I'm not going back to my apartment. I'll have somebody else clean that out and handle my stuff."

"When are you leaving for good?"

"I can't move in until Tuesday next week. Trying to coordinate this long distance has been a little bit of a pain in the ass, but I'll manage. I'll sleep on an air mattress if I have to for a few days."

"I gotta get back to Coconut Key. But I'd like to see you again before you go."

She looked at me, amused. "Would you?"

"Maybe," I said, downplaying my enthusiasm.

"I can think of worse things."

I laughed. "I bet you can."

"Let me know when you get a free minute to come back up."

"I will."

"Stay safe down there. Coconut Key has really gone to hell."

I chuckled. "Don't do anything stupid."

"Who me?"

"Stop poking the bear."

She gave me a mock salute. "Aye-aye, sir. No more poking."

Her tone didn't sound sincere.

I gave her a last passionate kiss goodbye, then left the B&B and hustled to the Porsche. I climbed inside, cranked up the engine, and headed back toward Coconut Key.

My phone buzzed halfway home. Jack's voice crackled through the speaker as the wind swirled around the cabin. "I've been snooping around this morning and discovered some interesting info."

"Do tell."

"Let's get to the important stuff first. How did it go last night?"

"Aside from someone trying to kill her, it went great."

"What!?"

I gave him the scoop.

"Well, that brings me to my second question. Is my car okay?"

I laughed. "It's still in one piece. I like it. I might not give it back."

"Maybe you should get your own."

"Why? I have access to yours?"

"The satisfaction of personal ownership."

"This is satisfying that urge just fine, and I don't have to pay for it," I teased.

He grumbled.

"What did you find out?"

"I paid a little visit to the marina at the *Trident Tower*. Julian's submarine is missing."

"Interesting."

"Talked to a few boaters in neighboring slips. A gentleman recalled a confrontation between Julian and a guy that matches the description of Eddie Everhart. Said the guy had a gun. You need to get your ass back here, and we need to talk to Eddie."

"I'll be there shortly," I said before ending the call.

Within half an hour, I was back at the marina. I hustled down the dock to the *Avventura* and changed clothes. Jack had taken Buddy out for his morning walk, so we were ready to start the day.

I called Isabella and asked her to pull the GPS data from Eddie's phone. Sure enough, he'd visited the marina at the *Trident Tower* the evening of Julian's death.

We drove to his apartment, and I put a heavy fist against the door. He greeted us with eager eyes. "What's going on? You have any leads?"

JD and I exchanged a knowing glance.

"Yeah," I said. "I think we do."

20

"You want to tell me what you were doing at the Trident Tower?"

Eddie's face tensed. "I just went over there to talk to him."

"Some of Julian's neighbors said the conversation was a little intense."

"You spoke with his neighbors?"

"That's what we do. We ask questions, generate leads."

"He took my sister out on that sub. He did something to her. He killed her and probably dumped her in the water. I wanted to look the scumbag in the eyes when I confronted him."

"Yeah, well, now he's dead."

"I heard." He paused. "You don't think I had something to do with that, do you?"

I gave an ominous shrug. "You certainly have a motive."

"What motive?"

"Oh, I don't know," I snarked. "You think he killed your sister? You confronted him. It's safe to say you have a lot of animosity toward the man. It wouldn't be unimaginable to think you killed him."

His face crinkled. "I didn't do anything."

"Do you own a gun, Eddie?"

His jaw tightened. "Yeah. Why?"

"What kind?"

"A 9mm."

"Can we see it?"

"What for?" he asked.

"Julian's neighbors said you had one when you confronted him."

His face wrinkled.

"You mind if we take a look around your apartment?" I asked.

"You got a warrant?"

"No."

"Then fuck off!" He slammed the door.

JD and I looked at each other.

"He seems a bit defensive," Jack said dryly.

We left the apartment and walked back to the Porsche.

JD theorized, "He goes over there and threatens Julian with a pistol. Forces him onto the sub. Shoots Julian while they are at sea, dumps the body, and scuttles the boat."

"How does he get back to the island?" I asked, climbing into the car.

JD slid behind the wheel. "Maybe he had someone pick him up."

"Who?"

Jack shrugged and started the engine.

"So you think that sub is sitting at the bottom of the ocean somewhere?"

"Could be. It's a pretty complex piece of machinery. I doubt he'd be able to pilot the thing."

"Let's go talk to your witness and get a sworn affidavit. See if we can get a warrant."

We headed over to the *Trident Tower* and found the gentleman JD had spoken with earlier. He had a 45-foot sportfishing boat in the slip next to the submarine. We found him in unit #1209. He answered the door after a few knocks, and JD introduced me. "Gene, this is my partner, Deputy Tyson Wild."

He extended his hand, and we shook.

"Gene Hawthorne. Good to know you."

"Likewise, sir," I said.

His hairline was at the crown of his head, and tufts of rusty gray hair sprouted on the sides. He had narrow, droopy brown eyes, saggy jowls, and his teeth were stained yellow.

He was early 70s, retired, and had a gravelly voice from years of smoking, though he had probably quit. I didn't smell it on him.

I pulled up a picture of Eddie on my phone and showed it to the man. "Is that the guy you saw confront Julian with a gun?"

Gene put on his tortoiseshell glasses and looked down his nose through the bifocals. "Yep. That's him, alright."

"Are you willing to make a sworn statement to that effect?"

"Whatever I can do to help. I didn't know Julian well, but he was always respectful to me. Hell, I thought that submarine of his was kind of fascinating. I was hoping to get a ride on it."

"What time was this?"

"In the evening. After sunset. I'd say, 7:30-ish."

"And you're sure Eddie had a gun?"

"That's the guy's name?"

I nodded.

"Yeah. He was yelling and cursing. Julian climbed out of the sub to talk to him on the top deck. This guy, Eddie, pulled a gun from his waistband and aimed it at Julian. Demanded to know where his sister was. Julian was surprisingly calm through the whole ordeal. He tried to de-escalate the situation. Told him he could search the boat. Fuck de-escalation! I broke out my shotgun and told the little fart to get going, or I'd put a hole in his ass. He took off after that," Gene said with a proud smirk.

"Why didn't you call the department?" I asked.

Gene shrugged. "Julian didn't want me to. Said the guy was probably all talk. He was sure the sister would turn up. Swore up and down, nothing bad happened to the girl on his watch."

"What happened after Eddie left?"

"I told Julian to watch his back. I hung around for a while to make sure the punk didn't come back, then I came up here."

"Did you see Eddie come back?"

"No, but that doesn't mean he didn't. I read in the paper that the coroner estimated Julian's time of death between midnight and 5 AM. That Eddie guy could have come back later. Julian was on that sub, tinkering with something all hours of the day and night. The guy was obsessed."

Gene made a statement, and we filled out an application for a warrant. Within the hour, Judge Echols approved it, and we returned to Eddie's apartment with a small tactical team.

I let JD do the honors. He banged on the door and shouted, "Coconut County! We have a warrant."

We'd been able to get in touch with the property manager. She joined us with a master key. I think Erickson and Faulkner were a little disappointed they didn't get to break the door down.

Before we put the key in the slot, Eddie pulled open the door with a scowl on his face. "Let's see the warrant."

I displayed it to him, and he looked it over briefly as the deputies pushed inside his apartment.

"This is bullshit. My sister gets abducted by that scumbag, and you're searching my apartment?"

"If you didn't do anything, you've got nothing to worry about."

"I didn't do anything."

The place was nice and well-kept. There was a small foyer that opened to the living room. There was a kitchen to the left and the master bedroom to the right. Sliding glass doors opened to a small terrace. He had a black leather sofa and black lacquer end tables. Magazines, a remote control, and a game controller sat atop a glass coffee table. There was a 65-inch flatscreen display on the entertainment center and cheap art on the walls—giclée reproductions from an online store.

We found the pistol in the nightstand by the bed, along with a box of 9mm ammunition. We confiscated both, bagged the evidence, and brought Eddie down to the station for questioning. We let him stew in the interrogation room for at least an hour.

"Am I under arrest?" he asked as we entered. "Can I go now?"

"We just have a few questions for you." He wasn't under arrest yet. He could leave anytime, but we didn't bother to make that clear. We could have charged him with assault or brandishing a firearm, but that would be tough to make stick. His words against Gene's.

"I understand what you're going through," I said.

His brow knitted. "No, you don't."

"You've got every right to be upset and angry. You confronted Julian. You left the marina, then came back. You forced Julian to take you out on the sub, and you shot him twice."

"No, I didn't."

"Eddie... Come on. We're gonna run ballistics on that pistol. It's gonna come up a match, and you're gonna get charged with murder."

His face was red. "No, I'm not."

"Tell me in detail what happened. Maybe we can get you involuntary manslaughter." I looked at JD and shrugged. "Heat of passion."

JD nodded.

"You weren't in your right mind," I continued. "You were grieving and filled with rage. You didn't go over there to kill him. Just to find out the truth."

"Now I'll agree with that. I just wanted to scare him and find out what happened to Evangeline."

"One thing led to another," I said. "Julian's dead. He had it coming," I said, trying to seem sympathetic.

"He had it coming, alright. But I didn't shoot him."

I frowned. "If you didn't kill him, who did?"

"How should I know? That's your job. Figure it out. But before you do that, figure out where my sister is. I want to know what he did with her. She's more important than him. Don't you dare focus your investigation on Julian."

"At this point in time, Evangeline is missing. We don't know if she's alive or dead."

"She's dead, and Julian killed her." His cheeks flushed, and sweat misted his skin. He asked again, "Am I under arrest? Can I go now?"

"You're free to go at any time," I said.

The chair screeched as he pushed away from the table and stood up. He marched to the door and banged on it. "Let me out of this motherfucker!"

I nodded to the video camera, and the guard buzzed him out.

We followed as he stormed away down the hall. We'd know soon enough if the ballistics matched.

21

"Brenda got the tox report back and the analysis on the cocaine," Denise said, joining us in the hallway outside the interrogation room. "You're not going to like this."

I groaned.

"There was enough fentanyl in that cocaine to kill an elephant. Several times the lethal amount in her system."

"We really need to find out where that stuff came from," JD said.

"There's one more thing," Denise said.

"She was about six weeks pregnant."

JD and I both cringed.

"That's a double homicide," JD said.

"Thanks for the heads up," I said.

"Anytime."

We left the station and headed to Oyster Avenue to grab lunch. We ate at *Royal Nirvana*. It was a casual spot, with plenty of outdoor seating on a red brick patio. Colorful umbrellas shaded the tables. It was an oasis of culinary delights.

We sat at the bar. In the evenings, a live band or singer/song-writer would take the stage.

Jack ordered the pan blackened Coconut Key shrimp, doused in butter and served with skillet corn, black beans, and rice. I went with the Jamaican Jerk Chicken with black beans and rice.

Paris Delaney's news report flashed on the screen halfway through the meal. "The tragic death of adult film star Tara DeVille has rocked the industry. Found dead of an apparent overdose aboard a superyacht belonging to local Coconut County deputies, the incident has raised questions."

I winced and groaned.

"The rising star was filming an upcoming movie, *Yacht Bunnies 2, All Access*, when the tragic incident took place. We attempted to speak with the cast and crew, but all declined to comment. Coconut County deputies also remained silent."

Paris cut to a clip of me walking down the dock, telling her she had her facts wrong.

"We also reached out to Sheriff Wayne Daniels for comment but didn't receive a response. We were able to get in touch with Violet Chase, Tara's best friend and co-star in several previous films."

The segment cut to a clip of a stunning brunette with creamy skin and a light dusting of freckles. Her azure eyes could certainly cast spells. Tears streamed down her sculpted cheeks. "She was such a wonderful person, inside and out. I can't believe she's gone."

"Did she have a history of drug abuse?" Paris asked.

Violet shook her head. "No. In all the time I've known her, I've never seen her do any drugs. She was such a kind soul."

JD and I exchanged a doubtful glance.

"In a bizarre twist," Paris said, "the body of Julian Pierce was also discovered floating in nearby waters. His body was recovered by sheriff's deputies at the time. As of this reporting, it is not clear if there is a connection between the two deaths."

Jack's face crinkled. "Oh, come on! There's clearly no connection. She's trying to milk this thing for all it's worth."

Paris always did have a flair for the dramatic, but this was taking it a bit far.

I wasn't exactly pleased with the angle she took with the story. I probably should have let well enough alone, but I decided to call her and give her an earful.

The ambitious blonde answered after a few rings.

"Why are you mischaracterizing this?"

"I'm not mischaracterizing anything. I'm reporting the facts as they are. You refused to give me a statement. I'm merely putting the pieces together."

"You're making it sound like we had some kind of involvement. The production company chartered the boat. Tara OD'd because she was snorting cocaine laced with fentanyl. We plan on finding out where that came from and getting it off the street."

"It's not my fault the facts of the case raise questions."

"That was a hit piece."

"It wasn't a hit piece. Are you willing to do an interview?"

"This is an ongoing investigation."

"I'm just doing my job," she said, attempting to absolve herself.

"I thought you wanted to elevate your reporting above salacious scandals."

"You're admitting this is scandalous?"

I gritted my teeth. "Paris!"

"You have to admit, the details are intriguing. Cocaine, adult entertainment, county deputies with a superyacht. It raises questions."

"No, *you're* raising questions. The wrong kind."

"There are no wrong questions. I'm offering you an opportunity to come on camera and explain your side of the story."

"I don't have to explain my side of the story to anybody."

"You're clearly concerned about appearances all of a sudden."

I balked, incredulous. "You're implying that there was some kind of impropriety going on. You throw around words like drugs and superyacht, and people start to wonder how two deputies can afford something like that. You know damn good and well we volunteer."

"Like I said, you're more than welcome to tell your side of it."

I stifled a growl.

"On a completely unrelated note, I guess now's not a good time to ask for a favor."

"No, it's not a good time."

I ended the call abruptly.

Just when I was starting to think she had redeeming qualities.

No sooner had I ended the call when Sheriff Daniels buzzed. "I'm assuming you saw that little exposé."

"I did."

"I'm already getting phone calls."

A resigned sigh escaped my lips. "What do you want me to do?"

22

"I should pull you two off the case," Daniels said.

My face tightened. I decided to try a little reverse psychology. "I think that's a great idea. Put somebody else on it. We could use the time off."

Daniels said nothing.

I was not about to drop the case, and Daniels knew it.

"I'm sure you can find somebody much more capable to work it."

His silence continued for a moment. "Keep quiet. Don't talk to her. That will only make it worse. In a few days, the news cycle will be on to something else." He paused. "In the meantime, find that dealer and get that crap off the street before someone else meets the same fate."

"We're on it," I said with a grin.

I ended the call.

We finished lunch, then tracked down Violet Chase. I called Denise and got her current address. She lived in the *Nautilus Tower*, another luxury high-rise with an attached marina. JD pulled to the valet, under the carport, and we hopped out. He gave the guy a nice tip and asked him to keep it up front.

I flashed my badge through the glass door, and the concierge buzzed us in.

Much like the Trident, the Nautilus had an opulent lobby with a waterfall, a baby grand piano, a lounge area, and plenty of plants. There was an array of amenities. The rent wasn't cheap. Violet Chase must have been doing well.

We took the elevator up to the 16th floor, walked the hallway, and banged on #1622.

A plain-looking brunette in her early 20s answered the door. She was dressed in a tank top and jeans and didn't have make-up on. A small DSLR camera hung from her grasp. "Can I help you?"

I flashed my badge and made introductions. "We're looking for Violet Chase."

She shouted down the foyer. "Violet, two cops are looking for you."

The girl looked at us with disdain.

Violet appeared at the end of the hallway, wearing skimpy lingerie. She could definitely quicken your pulse.

"We have a few questions for you about Tara DeVille."

"Please, come in."

We stepped into the foyer, and the brunette closed the door behind us.

Violet introduced us. "This is my assistant, Rachel. We were just in the middle of a photo shoot for my *For the Fans*."

It was an online website where content creators could charge monthly subscriptions in exchange for exclusive photo sets and videos.

The living room had been converted in to a photography studio. Background stands held 9-foot rolls of colored paper that could be rolled down with ease—white, gray, pink, and chroma-key green. Lights in soft boxes provided flattering, even lighting. There was another DSLR video camera on a tripod. At the other end of the living room, there was a desk with a dual monitor editing set up. Several sexy outfits hung from a rolling clothes rack, and there was a bin of props nearby. Everything a cosplayer would need.

"This is quite the home studio," JD said.

"Thank you. I'm building a little empire online. I told Tara she should do the same thing. Why work for a guy like Don Jammer for pennies when you can work for yourself and make millions?"

Not everyone could do it, but if you had a little business savvy, great content, and marketing expertise, a pretty girl could make a ton of money creating lewd content for lonely men on the Internet.

"We saw your interview with Paris Delaney and thought you might have valuable insight into Tara's situation," I said.

Violet frowned, and her eyes misted. "She was my best friend."

"Tell me who her dealer was."

Violent hesitated.

Rachel excused herself from the conversation and moved to the editing station. She downloaded the recent footage they had shot and started organizing the images.

"I don't know. Tara was a good girl. She didn't normally do drugs."

I gave her a flat look. "I know you're trying to protect your friend's image. But something tells me this wasn't the first time she'd dabbled with cocaine."

Violet glanced at Rachel, then back to us. I got the impression she wasn't comfortable speaking about her friend with an extra pair of ears in the room. "Rachel, would you be a doll and get me a venti latte?"

"Sure. You want anything else while I'm out?"

"Something for lunch. Something healthy."

"Any suggestions?"

"Surprise me."

Rachel excused herself and left the condo.

"You were saying?"

Violet took a breath. "I really don't want Tara to be characterized as just another stupid slut who OD'd. She was much more than a porn star or whatever they will say about her."

"I'm sure she was. We are all more than the labels people give us."

A sad look tightened her face. "That's so true." She paused. "Andy Trainor. But you didn't get the name from me."

"That's her dealer?"

"That's everybody's dealer in this business. His prices are reasonable, he's discrete, and he delivers. You don't have to go to any sketchy apartment in *Jamaica Village*. But it doesn't make sense. Andy's got top-notch stuff." She realized what she was admitting to. "Not that I ever did the stuff."

"Of course not."

"Do you think he just didn't know what was in it?"

Dealers cut their product for all kinds of reasons. Usually to stretch the amount and make more money. Sometimes they think people will get a better high if they add in potent substances like fentanyl, but that's usually added to heroin to give it more punch. Fentanyl and cocaine can be a dangerous cocktail. Uppers and downers.

A look of panic washed over Violet's face. "Do you think other people might have the same stuff?"

"If he sold it to Tara, it's likely he sold it to other people as well."

Her face tightened.

"You don't have any around, do you?"

"No," she said, not doing a great job of sounding innocent.

"Are you sure?"

She nodded.

"We can't bring your friend back, but you can help us save more lives."

"How?"

23

"I don't know if I can do that," Violet said.

"It's just a simple call or text," I said.

"Yeah, but he'll know I set him up."

"No, he won't. Not yet, anyway. We'll make the buy. You just get him over here and make the introduction."

Her mouth scrunched up as she thought about it.

"You could be saving someone's life," I added.

"What do I say?"

"Just tell him you're with two friends, and you need party favors. Ask him how soon he can get here?"

She hesitated another moment, then finally agreed. She pulled out her cell phone and sent Andy a text.

He replied a few minutes later. *[How much do you need?]*

Violet looked at me for guidance.

"An eight ball," I whispered.

It was street slang for 3.5 grams, or 1/8 of an ounce.

She replied. A moment later, Andy gave her a price. I told her that was acceptable. Andy replied that he would be at her condo in 20 minutes.

We hung out in the living room, and JD set up his cell phone to film the exchange.

JD couldn't help but admire Violet's studio. He asked about her photography setup, and she told us about her budding empire. She told us how much she was pulling in a month, and the figure was staggering.

"Why would anyone work for a guy like Don?" JD asked.

Violet shrugged. "I don't know. And I don't even have to sleep with anyone on camera. I just post naughty pictures, play with toys, and play video games in a hot tub while wearing a bikini or nothing at all. But it's full-time work. I'm streaming on camera almost 12 hours a day. Everyday. Doesn't leave much time for a social life."

"I bet your boyfriend doesn't like that," JD said, fishing.

"I don't have a boyfriend. No time. Besides, most guys can't handle this," she said, motioning to her surroundings. "It's a 24/7 production. Most guys want a girl who's available at their beck and call. That ain't me. I've got a window of opportunity here, and I'm trying to maximize my earning potential."

"Gotta make hay while the sun is shining."

"Exactly," she said with a smile, connecting with JD.

Rachel returned with the coffee. Violet pulled her aside and filled her in. "Do not mention that these two are cops when Andy is here."

"Why? Are you setting him up?"

"No."

She didn't buy it. "Look, I just work here. I don't know anything. And the less I know, the better."

"Good."

A few minutes later, Andy knocked on the door.

JD started recording.

Rachel answered and escorted Andy into the living room. Violet greeted him with a hug and a smile, then introduced us. "I'd like you to meet Tyson and his friend, Jack."

Andy surveyed us with curious eyes.

We shook his hand, and there was an awkward moment as we sized each other up.

He was a skinny guy about 6 feet tall with curly blond hair. He had a slim face, blue eyes, and a little bit of sandy stubble. His eyes narrowed at JD. "I know you from somewhere."

Before JD could speak, Violet interrupted. "He's in the business. You've probably seen one of his movies. Jack Slammer."

I stifled a smirk.

Andy looked at Jack. "Sorry, bro. I don't pay attention to the guys."

"We're just props, anyway," JD said.

"He's got a big prop," Violet said.

Jack grinned with pride.

If I didn't know better, I'd say she was flirting with JD.

I pulled out a wad of cash, and Andy pulled out the eight ball. We made the exchange, quick and clean.

"You want to sample it?" he asked.

"I trust you. If Violet says you're good, then you're good. Besides, I'm saving it for later tonight. Let me get your digits in case I need more."

We exchanged numbers, then Andy said his goodbyes and left.

Jack ended the recording and slipped his phone into his pocket.

After Andy was gone, Violet asked, "That's it?"

"That's it."

"You not going to bust him?"

"I'll bring this to the lab and see what's what," I said, dangling the baggie of crunchy white powder. "Either way, we've got enough to make an arrest at a later date."

I gave her my card and thanked her for her cooperation.

Jack gave her a card as well. "Just in case you need anything."

She smiled. There was potential in that smile.

Violet escorted us to the door, and we said our goodbyes again.

Jack strutted the hallway with an accomplished grin.

We headed back to the station, logged the evidence, and filled out after-action reports. Then it was time for band practice.

We met the guys at the warehouse and ran through the setlist. Jack had planned a New Year's Eve bash on the boat, and the band was going to play an unplugged set. After practice, we knocked back a few drinks at *Volcanic*.

I called Kyra to check in on her. She didn't answer.

24

Brenda called in the morning as I was grilling breakfast in the galley. Bacon sizzled and the smell of coffee permeated the air. "Bad news. Ballistics on Eddie's gun don't match. You might be looking for a different shooter."

"Thanks for the heads up."

"Who knows? Maybe he had another weapon and tossed it. I'll let you guys figure that out."

Jack staggered into the galley as I ended the call. I filled him in on the details.

We chowed down on the sky deck. After breakfast, we set out to find Julian's friend Garrison. I figured he might have a little insight. He lived on a 45-foot sailboat in Pirates' Cove. It was a 2003 *Barzetti*. It was well maintained. He had installed solar panels for power on the go.

I banged on the hull, and Garrison poked his head out of the cockpit a moment later. I flashed my badge to jog his memory. "I'd like to talk to you about Julian."

A frown tugged his face, and he shook his head. "I can't believe he's dead."

"You have any idea where the submarine might be?"

"No. Do you have any suspects?"

"We do, but that's not exactly panning out right now. Since you helped build it, I'm assuming you're intimately familiar with the craft."

He nodded. "I know that submarine like the back of my hand."

"How difficult was it to navigate?"

"On the surface, simple. Julian designed it for ease of use. A joystick to navigate and simple throttle control. Underwater, that's a different story. You'd have to know what you are doing. Especially if something goes wrong."

"So, you think an average person could sail the vessel on the surface, no problem?"

"Anybody with a little boating experience, probably. Why?"

I told him our theory.

Garrison shook his head. "I think somebody shot Julian, stole the boat, and dumped him in the water."

"Why do you think that?"

"Seems easier than forcing Julian to take the sub out."

"Why steal the sub?"

He looked at us like we were idiots. "It's a functioning submarine. You know how valuable one of those things is!? There are a lot of people that would love to get their hands on a transoceanic submarine. I don't have to spell it out for you, do I?"

JD and I exchanged a glance. We knew exactly what he was getting at.

"Was Julian involved in anything shady?"

"No!" he said with a wrinkled brow. "Julian's ego may have gotten the best of him at times, but he was by the book."

"Except for when it came to his marriage," I snarked.

Garrison gave me a look.

"Did he talk to you at all about Evangeline?"

"I told you the other day. He took her out, said they hooked up, and he brought her back."

"I believe Kent told us that. You told him to be quiet."

Garrison's face tensed. "You were harassing a dear friend. Forgive me for being protective."

"Do you know anyone else who may have wanted to harm him besides Evangeline's brother?"

Garrison shrugged.

"I know he was going through a pretty contentious divorce," I said.

"That's an understatement. You think Gwen might be involved? Spouses are always suspects, right?"

I nodded.

Garrison shook his head in disgust. "I bet that bitch is doing a happy dance now that Julian's gone."

"Was it that bad?"

"Worse." He paused. "Maybe she got her boyfriend to get rid of Julian."

"Boyfriend?"

He frowned. "Yeah, she's dating some young punk. This sure makes life a lot easier for her. She gets to keep all her money."

"Her money?"

"Yeah. Gwen is loaded. The house, the cars, the submarine. That's all Gwen's money. I guess she didn't like Julian spending it."

"I'm sure she didn't like him spending it at *Forbidden Fruit*."

"She's no saint, either."

"You know her boyfriend's name?"

"Flint Foster. Total loser. He bartends at *Panic*. Julian thought she was fooling around, so he hired a private investigator."

"What's the investigator's name?"

"I don't know."

I thanked him for the info.

"Listen, if there's anything I can do, let me know," Garrison said.

"I will."

"Keep me posted. I sure hope you get whoever is responsible. Julian had a lot to contribute to the world. We lost someone special."

I gave him my card and told him I might have additional questions.

We walked from the dock back to the parking lot. I called Isabella. "I need another favor."

"You and your favors."

"You love it. It keeps you entertained."

She sighed.

"Look at the GPS history for Gwen and a guy named Flint Foster. See if you can put them near the marina at the *Trident Tower* the night of Julian's death."

"Anybody else you want me to look into?"

"I'll send you texts as things develop."

"I'm here to serve your every need," she said, her voice thick with sarcasm.

We hopped into the Porsche and drove to the *Platinum Dunes*. I tried calling Kyra again along the way. I was starting to get worried.

It went to voicemail.

"Hey, you're either avoiding me, or you've been assassinated. If you've been assassinated, have your ghost give me a sign so I can stop worrying. If you're avoiding me, just say so."

"Direct and to the point," JD said after I ended the call.

"Direct is best."

"That night must have been memorable."

"We had a good time," I said in an understated tone.

We drove to the fancy neighborhood and found Gwen's McMansion. We hustled to the door, and I rang the video doorbell.

There was no answer.

Her car was in the driveway. A moment later, a guy's voice crackled through the speaker. "What do you want?"

I flashed my badge to the lens. "Deputy Wild with Coconut County. I'd like to have a word with Gwen."

"She's not here right now."

It sounded like we'd woken him up.

"Is this Flint?" I said, hazarding a guess.

He stammered, "Yeah. Who are you?"

I reintroduced myself. "Do you have a minute to talk?" I tried to make it sound casual.

25

"I didn't really know the guy," Flint said.

"You're living in his house," JD said.

"It's not his house anymore, is it? Besides, Gwen paid for it."

Flint stood in the doorway. He was 6'1" with sandy blond hair that hung to his shoulders. He had a square jaw lined with a week's worth of stubble. His ice-blue eyes and low brow gave him a mysterious quality that I'm sure the ladies found intriguing.

"How long have you two been seeing each other?" I asked.

"I don't see how that's any of your business."

"Did you ever have any altercations with Julian?"

"I told you, I didn't know the guy."

"It's my understanding he knew about you."

His eyes narrowed. "How?"

"Where were you the night Julian was murdered?"

Flint thought about it for a moment. "I worked until midnight, then came here."

"Did you go by the Trident Tower?"

"No. Why would I go there?"

"Do you own a gun?"

His brow knitted. "No."

"What about Gwen?"

He shrugged. "I don't know. What are you getting at?"

"I'm just thinking Julian's death makes it a little more convenient for you two."

His jaw flexed. "What do you mean, convenient?"

"Is it serious between you two?"

"Yeah. We're getting married."

"Like I said, with Julian gone, that paves the way."

"So?"

"Seems fortuitous for you."

"What?"

"Lucky," I explained.

"I guess. You can't expect me to shed a tear for the guy. Sucks for him, but honestly, now that you mention it, I'm thrilled about it. I can quit my job, and we don't have to sneak around anymore."

"Doesn't look like you're sneaking around."

He frowned at me. "Look, I didn't kill Julian, and neither did Gwen."

"You mind if we look around?"

"For what?"

"A 9mm pistol."

"Are you serious with this shit?"

"Yeah, I'm pretty serious."

"Man, fuck off! Get a warrant." He slammed the door.

"I'm kind of thinking he doesn't like us," JD said.

"What gave you that idea?" I asked dryly.

We walked back to the Porsche and climbed in.

Jack's phone buzzed. He pulled the device from his pocket and took the call. "Hey, Zach?"

Zach's voice crackled through the speaker, but I couldn't decipher it.

"That's great!" JD said. "We're on our way."

He ended the call and slipped the phone back into his pocket.

"What was that about?"

Jack grinned. "You'll see."

He cranked up the engine, and we headed back to the marina at *Diver Down*. He parked the Spyder, and I followed Jack as he hustled down the dock and waited at the empty slip that used to be home to our wake boat.

Jack waited eagerly, staring out past the breakwater.

It wasn't long before a sleek 27-foot 275 XTX Yamazuki appeared. It had a slate gray hull with white trim and a molded-in hard top. The svelte, angular craft sliced through the water with ease.

"Ordered it online," JD muttered.

Zach Forster was at the helm. He waved as he drew near. He was a local dealer that we had done plenty of business with.

Zach pulled into the slip, and we tied off the lines.

"Here she is!" he said with a beaming smile.

We marveled at the new boat.

It weighed in at 5,800 pounds with a 9' beam and a draft of 22". Yacht-certified seating capacity and all the amenities you could imagine in a boat like this. There was an integrated swim platform, cushioned and bolstered luxury seats, sun pads at the stern, plenty of storage, a dinette table, a galley with sink and spray shower, touch screen display, push-button start/stop, throttled by wire, a pumping stereo system, and twin supercharged mega vortex high output engines with 2000cc of displacement each. It had stainless steel bow rails and a hardtop with a panoramic, dimmable skylight.

It was a lot like our old wake boat, only much nicer. The pinnacle of luxury in its class.

"What do you think?" Zach asked.

"I think it looks great," JD said.

Zach handed the keys to Jack. It was basically a wireless fob that provided keyless operation. As long as the fob was within range, the boat would operate.

"We just need to do a little paperwork, and you're good to go," Zach said.

Once JD had signed for delivery, Zach shook our hands and congratulated us. "Enjoy, gentlemen! Let me know if you need anything else."

He called a rideshare and hustled down the dock to the parking lot.

We walked to *Diver Down* and took a seat at the bar.

Teagan greeted us with a warm smile. She read our expressions right away. "What's that look?"

"New toy," JD said with a grin.

He told her about the boat.

"I want a ride!"

"Anytime."

"You boys hungry?"

"I could eat," JD said.

Teagan grabbed a few menus. "How are the investigations going?"

"Eh," I groaned.

"You'll figure it out," she said in a cheery tone.

Denise called as we surveyed the menu. "I hate to throw a wrench in your investigation, but that coke you logged into evidence from Andy Trainer... it's 96% pure. No traces of fentanyl."

"You gotta be kidding me."

"That's what the lab says. It's about as pure as pure can get."

A frustrated sigh escaped my lungs. "Thanks for the info."

She ended the call, and I updated JD.

"Maybe Tara got the coke somewhere else."

"Maybe somebody gave it to her," I said.

"On purpose?"

"Could be."

"Oh, my God!" Teagan exclaimed. "It's just like that movie."

"What movie?" I asked.

"*Tomorrow She Dies*. You have to see it. It's SO good."

"So, what happens?"

"I'm not going to tell you spoilers."

I gave her a flat look.

She raised her hands innocently. "Okay, but don't blame me. You asked for this."

"Spill it," I said, growing impatient.

"Okay, in the movie, a girl poisons her sister by lacing her coke with fentanyl so she can *console* her sister's grieving husband."

"Some sister," JD muttered.

"Maybe the movie sparked somebody's imagination."

"Copying a murder method doesn't sound very imaginative," I said.

Teagan frowned at me. "Well, you know what I mean."

I was of the mind that movies didn't cause people to do things they didn't have in them anyway. But it might give them a few ideas about how to do it.

I called Violet. She answered after a few rings. Her nervous voice filtered through the speaker in my phone, "Did you arrest Andy?"

"Not yet."

"I'm so freaked out he's gonna learn I sold him out."

"I'll give you a heads up before we arrest him."

"Did you test the drugs he sold you?"

"No trace of fentanyl."

"Oh, thank God!" Then she covered, "I mean, that no one else will get hurt."

She clearly had a stash of Andy's stuff somewhere.

"Could Tara have gotten the drugs from somewhere else?"

She hesitated. "I guess."

"Did she use any other dealers that you know about?"

"She'd been buying from Andy for a while. Somebody else on set could have given it to her, but nobody else has OD'd, right?

"No. Not yet." I paused. "Can you think of anyone who wanted her out of the picture?"

"You mean out of the movie they were filming, or... dead?"

"Dead."

"You think she was murdered?"

"I'm beginning to think that's a possibility," I said.

"Well, she didn't get along with Sydney Voss at all."

"I gathered. Any reason for that besides professional jealousy?"

"You know, some personality types just don't mix. I think she was starting to take a lot of jobs away from her. Sydney is sort of aging out of the business."

"She's not that old."

"Well, she's getting into MILF territory."

"Was Tara seeing anyone else besides Billy?" I asked.

Violet hesitated. "Well, Tara was pretty much a free spirit."

"I take that to mean she wasn't exactly faithful."

"You're not going to tell Billy any of this, are you? He'll be heartbroken."

"Not unless it becomes relevant to the case."

"I really feel for the guy. He was so in love with Tara. But, you know, in this business, it can be hard to be in a committed relationship. It's a fine line. I mean, having sex with somebody on camera isn't cheating, but the same act *is* when the camera isn't rolling? It's acting, right? But you kinda have to jump through a few mental hoops to justify it."

"Who else was she seeing?"

"She had a little thing with Dick Steele."

"They seemed like they had chemistry," I said.

"I think she really liked him. And I know Dick had a thing with Sydney at one point, so that increased the tension between the two."

"Did Billy know about her affair with Mr. Steele?"

"I'm not sure, but I think he suspected."

"Was there anybody else?"

She groaned. "I hate to say it, but she was sleeping with Joey Bangs, too."

"The director?"

"She wanted a role in his horror movie. Tara thought she could break out of adult film. She thought Joey's horror movie would be her entrée into legitimate acting."

"Anybody else?"

"I'm making my friend sound bad, but... Don Jammer."

"*That* guy?"

"She wanted to keep getting cast in his pictures."

"Is that standard procedure? Does every actress that wants a role in Don's films have to do that?"

"Well, Don holds casting sessions to find new talent. You want to see how somebody performs before you put them on camera."

"That's quite a list of romantic partners. I can see a lot of potential conflicts and motives developing."

"There's somebody else." She said, almost cringing.

"Who?" I asked.

"You can't tell anyone I told you this. You have to promise me."

"I'll be discreet. But this is a criminal investigation."

"Logan Shea."

That hung there for a moment.

"*The* Logan Shea?"

"Yep."

Logan was a movie star with a wholesome, clean-cut image. He had a wife and two kids. He had a multi-picture deal with a major studio that produced family-oriented content. If word got out he was having a tawdry affair with a porn star, the tabloids would have a field day. He'd lose his contract with the studio. Millions of dollars were at stake.

"Are you sure about that?"

"Positive."

I paused, processing the information. "Did you know that Tara was pregnant?"

Violet gasped. "No. She never said anything."

"I'm not sure she knew."

"How far along was she?"

I told her.

"Any idea who the father might be?" I asked.

"Your guess is as good as mine."

I had quite the list to choose from.

I thanked her for the info and ended the call.

"I'm beginning to think this was no accidental overdose," JD said.

We chowed down on lunch. Kyra called midway. I swiped the screen and held the phone to my ear. "I take it you're still alive?"

"No. This is my ghost haunting you."

I chuckled.

"Sorry, I've been out of pocket. My SAC insisted that I change locations after the incident, and I left my phone charger at the bed-and-breakfast."

"A likely story."

"Now, why would I want to avoid you? I'm trying to think of a legitimate excuse to see you again without sounding too desperate."

"I think that could be arranged."

"I don't want to make this a regular thing. But since I am leaving town, I might as well make the most of it. That is, if you think you won't get too attached."

I laughed again. She had a certain quality that was addictive. "Got plans for New Year's?"

"Well, there's been a slight change of plans. I talked to the manager of that apartment complex in Houston. They were able to get that unit turned around and ready for move-in early. I'm flying out New Year's Eve day."

I wasn't thrilled to hear that. "It's probably for the best. Safer."

"I was thinking, if you've got time, maybe you could come up here. We could order in and ring in the new year a little early."

"I'd like that."

"Good. Think you can make it up here tonight by 7 PM?"

"I have a few suspects to interview, but that should be doable. Where are you staying?"

"I'll send you the details on Memo."

Memo was an encrypted messaging app.

I ended the call, and JD gave me a curious look.

"Careful, she could be habit-forming."

"You got that right."

We finished eating, then tracked down Sydney Voss.

26

We walked onto the set of another Don Jammer production with Joey Bangs at the helm. This project was less ambitious than *Yacht Bunnies 2*. They'd rented a cabana at the *Seven Seas*.

The plot was pretty basic. Sydney played a recent divorcee taking a vacation to write her steamy romance novel. After years in a sexless marriage, she explored her desires and chronicled them in her novel. In this particular scene, Dick Steele played the bellhop, and got an extra special tip when he delivered her bags to the room. Or, more accurately, she got the tip. And then some.

Moans of ecstasy filtered out of the cabana, and I figured it wouldn't take long for neighboring guests on their family vacation to complain.

"Can you make it quick?" Don said. "I don't want to keep you from doing your job, but I'd like to get my shots before we get kicked out of here."

We spoke to Don in the living room while the action raged in the bedroom.

"This won't take long. We just have a few questions for you and some of your crew," I said.

"Me?" he asked with raised eyebrows.

"It's my understanding you were having a sexual relationship with the deceased."

He tucked his chin and looked around like it was a silly question. "I gotta audition a girl before she gets in front of the camera. What does that have to do with anything? She OD'd. I don't know where she got the drugs. I didn't give them to her. I don't like my talent on that shit. It makes them unreliable."

"Did Tara have to audition for every part?"

Don's eyes narrowed at me. "She was a rising star in high demand. She didn't have to do anything she didn't want to do."

"We're not so sure it was an accident," I said.

I explained the situation to him.

He looked stunned.

"It's imperative we find the source of those drugs. You wouldn't want more of your talent to succumb to the same fate."

"You think this may have been deliberate?"

I shrugged. "Could be."

"I liked Tara. I made a lot of money off her." He leaned in and whispered, "Her movies get more viewers than Sydney's."

Moans still filtered out of the bedroom.

"Can you think of anyone who might have wanted her dead?"

He raised his hands innocently. "I don't know. Maybe you ought to talk to the people who stand to benefit from her passing."

He was throwing Sydney under the bus without naming names.

The scene wrapped up in the bedroom, and Joey Bangs yelled cut.

Sydney emerged from the bedroom a few moments later, looking exhausted and disheveled, her skin slick with sweat. She wore absolutely nothing at all, prancing around like it was no big deal.

JD and I tried not to stare.

Tried.

She didn't look thrilled to see us. "What are you doing here?"

"A few additional questions for you," I said.

"For me?"

"And the other crew members who were on set that day."

That seemed to set her at ease somewhat.

"Would you like a moment to get dressed?"

She smirked and arched her chest, displaying her store-bought endowments. "Why? Does my body make you uncomfortable?"

"No. Not at all."

"How can I help you?"

The director, cinematographer, and lighting guy set up the next scene. Joey surveyed the area, putting together a game plan. He had a discussion with Don. "I'm thinking she has a leaky faucet and calls hotel maintenance."

"That's original," Don said dryly.

"Okay, she loses an earring down the sink."

"I don't care how you get them naked in the kitchen, just get them naked."

"Perhaps we should speak in private," I said to Sydney.

We stepped through the sliding glass door onto the patio. It was surrounded by greenery, and a path led down to the private white sand beach. Teal waves crashed against the shore.

"We're concerned that other people may be in jeopardy," I said to Sydney as JD slid the door shut behind us.

Her brow knitted. "What do you mean?"

I gave her the details on the tainted drugs.

She looked shocked. "That's terrible! Who would do such a thing?"

"That's what we're trying to find out. You sure you don't know where Tara acquired the cocaine?"

"I told you, I'm clean. I don't mess with that shit."

"You don't know where she got it?"

Sydney shook her head.

"You didn't give it to her, right?"

"Absolutely not," she said, growing irritated.

"If any more of that coke is floating around the set, I'd hate for someone to—"

"If there was more floating around the set, someone else would have died by now."

"Are you saying there's been more drug use since Tara's death?"

Sydney laughed. "What do you think?"

"Who?"

"I work with these people. I'm not going to rat them out."

"One of your coworkers may be a murderer."

She gave me a doubtful look. "That's a bit of a stretch, don't you think? Tara got hold of some bad shit, probably from a shady dealer. It happens. Goes with the territory. Buyer beware, right?"

Other hotel guests walked by the beach. A man caught sight of Sydney, and his eyes popped out of their sockets.

His wife wasn't so enthused. Her face twisted into a scowl, and she smacked his arm as hard as she could. He winced with pain and stopped looking. They kept walking, and he gave a quick glance back to soak up another look.

It was amazing how fast we'd grown accustomed to talking to a naked woman on the patio.

"It seems like your career is doing well," I said.

"It is. I'm booked solid for the rest of the week. There's been a sudden spike in demand."

"You know, some people might be inclined to think that's a motive," I said.

"Well, then, some people are way off base."

"Is there any offscreen chemistry between you and Dick Steele?"

"I don't see how that's relevant."

I shrugged. "Just curious."

"Dick is a friend. Sometimes Dick is more than a friend."

"Did it bother you that Tara was sleeping with your *friend*?"

"I watched them have sex on camera all the time. It didn't bother me. We have no obligation to each other."

Joey slid open the door. "Sydney, you're up again in five minutes."

Sydney smiled. "Gentlemen, if you'll excuse me, I need to get into character."

She slipped inside.

As Joey closed the door, I said, "Can we get a word with you?"

27

"I'm clean," Joey said. "I've got a career. I don't mess with that shit."

"You know, I've been hearing that a lot lately," I said. "But Tara had to get the drugs from somewhere."

"I don't know what to tell you. She didn't get them from me."

"You two had a thing, right?"

His face tightened. "We hooked up here and there."

"Did Billy know?"

"He would have flipped out if he knew. He's a little possessive."

"Most people don't like sharing their significant other," I said.

"Goes with the turf in this biz."

"Don't you guys worry about…?"

"Everybody gets tested on a regular basis. It's a small community. We're all safe."

"What happens when someone goes outside the community?"

"That's when it gets dangerous." He paused. "Listen, I've got a movie to make."

"Sure, just a few more quick questions. Were you going to cast Tara in your horror film?"

"I was going to give her a small role."

"What about Sydney?"

"She's taking over Tara's part."

"Good to know," I said. "You know Andy Trainer, right?"

"Yeah."

"Who's his competition?"

"Like I said, I don't mess with that stuff. I really gotta get back to work."

"I understand. Could you send Mr. Steele out here to speak with us? We will be brief," I assured.

Joey frowned and slipped back inside.

"Talk about a tangled web," JD said.

Dick stepped onto the patio a few moments later, his moneymaker swinging in the breeze. "You guys wanted to talk to me?"

I ran through all the same questions and got the same answers. He didn't do drugs and didn't know where Tara had gotten the coke from. Either everyone on the set was on the straight and narrow, or somebody was telling tall tales.

"How serious was your relationship with Tara?" I asked.

He paused, then frowned. "I really liked her. She was a cool chick."

"So, it was just a casual thing?"

He is eyes misted. "Not for me, man. It was more than casual. I *really* liked her."

"Did Billy know about you two?"

He shrugged. "She was planning on breaking up with him."

I lifted a surprised brow. "Why bother if she was doing whatever she wanted on the side?"

"I think she felt bad about it. She told Billy that they weren't exclusive, but he didn't want to hear it. That's why she kept a lot of things from him."

"What else did she keep from him?"

"I don't know."

"Did you know she was pregnant?"

His eyes rounded. "What!?"

"Yep."

"I guess it could be mine. But..." He frowned and shook his head. "Man, that's fucked up."

"You see why we want to find out where she was getting her supply? Two lives were lost."

"Seriously, I don't know. I didn't even know she was using that day."

"How regular of a thing was it for her?" I asked.

He shrugged again.

"You two were close, but you didn't notice her drug use?" I said, skeptical of the claim.

"I've found that people can be really good about hiding addictions."

I couldn't argue there. A lot of people could hide things up until the point where they couldn't. Then, all of a sudden, catastrophe.

"Did you know Tara was seeing Logan Shea?"

Dick's eyes rounded with shock. "Really? *That* guy?"

"That guy," I confirmed.

"Huh. News to me." He looked a little bothered by it.

"Guess she kept a lot of stuff from you, too."

"Seems like it." He looked distraught.

Two girls on the beach noticed Mr. Steele. They made their way up the path and hovered near the patio, giddy with excitement.

"Oh my God, it's you!" One of them shouted. "You're Dick Steele!"

Dick grinned.

"Oh my God! Can we get an autograph?"

"Certainly," Dick said, eager to please his female fans.

They rushed to join us on a patio. One of them pulled out their phone and handed it to me. "Will you take our picture?"

The girls gathered on either side of the porn star and made obscene gestures as I snapped the photo. Her friend gave me her cell phone, wanting one as well. I took another picture.

"What are your names?" Dick asked, eyeing his fans like they were an all-you-can-eat buffet.

"I'm Kathy, and this is Megan."

The girls pawed on Mr. Steele, telling him all about their fantasies.

Dick was happy to listen.

Joey slid open the glass door. "Pictures up. We're ready to roll."

"Can we watch?" one of the girls asked.

Dick shrugged. "Talk to the director."

"How old are you girls?" Joey asked.

"19."

"I need to see some ID."

They broke out their driver's licenses' and after a quick evaluation, Joey escorted them inside. "So, have you ever thought about doing adult entertainment?"

We followed them inside and left as security was knocking. I pulled open the door on the way out, and Carl, the head of security, gave me a quizzical look. He helped us out on a few cases before.

"We're investigating a case," I assured.

"Oh, okay. We got complaints about... public nudity."

Don hovered in the foyer behind me. "No worries. Won't happen again."

"Look, I don't care what goes on in the hotel room. Just don't let it spill out into the common areas," Carl said.

We left the cabana and walked with Carl down the path toward the parking lot. He'd seen the news report, and we caught him up to speed.

We left the hotel to find Logan Shea. He had a second home in Coconut Key and lived in the upscale neighborhood of *Stingray Bay*. I wasn't sure if he was even in town, but it was worth a shot.

28

I rang the video doorbell at Logan Shea's mansion.

A voice crackled through the speaker a moment later. "Whatever you're selling, I don't want any. There's no soliciting in this neighborhood."

I flashed my badge to the lens. "Coconut County. We'd like to speak with Logan Shea."

"What's this about?" Logan asked.

"We thought you might be able to provide some information about a recently deceased individual."

"I don't know anybody who's died recently."

"Tara DeVille."

Static crackled over the line as he went silent for a moment.

"I don't have a comment."

"Might want to talk to us before the story hits the press."

"What story?"

"You know, the one about your tawdry affair."

He was silent again.

"What do you want?" he asked. "Is this some kind of shakedown?"

"No shakedown. We just need to ask you a few questions."

"Do I need a lawyer?"

"I don't know. Is there some reason you would need a lawyer? Because if you need a lawyer, I'm going to get suspicious."

"No. I don't need a lawyer. Hang on. I'll be there in a minute."

The speaker crackled as the call disconnected.

JD and I exchanged a curious glance.

Logan pulled open the door a moment later. He was in his mid-30s, but still had that boyish charm. Good looking, square jaw, dimple in the chin, piercing blue eyes, dark wavy hair. He was a child star that had managed to transition into adulthood seamlessly. He kept his reputation clean until now. Concern filled his eyes as they flicked between the two of us. "You two don't look like cops. Let's see your badges again."

I displayed mine for him. "It's real."

"Look, my wife is out shopping with the kids. Can we wrap this up before they get back? I don't want them to get alarmed."

"What would they get alarmed about?"

He laid the sarcasm on thick. "Oh, I don't know. It's totally normal for cops to show up at my door asking about a dead porn star."

"Tell me about the extent of your relationship with Tara."

His jaw tightened. "You're not recording this, are you?"

"No."

"Have you seen her?"

"Yeah. Pretty girl."

"What was I going to do? Turn that down. Fuck of a lifetime, bro."

Did you know she was doing cocaine?"

His eyes narrowed at me like it was a stupid question. "No. I had no idea."

More sarcasm.

"You know where she got it from?"

"Her dealer, I suppose."

"Did you ever do coke with her?"

"I don't have to answer that."

"I'll take that as a *yes*," I said.

"Take it however you want."

"Did you ever give her your drugs?"

"No."

I didn't suspect he'd admit to it if he did.

"Look, we hung out a few times. Had fun. That was it. Sucks that she died. But I can't be anywhere near this thing. You understand."

"Sure. I just need to find out who her dealer is so we can get that stuff off the street before anybody else gets hurt."

He hesitated for a moment. "There was a guy who supplied her." He tried to think of his name.

"Andy?"

"Yeah, that's it."

"Did you know she was pregnant?"

He looked astonished. "No. Are you sure?"

I nodded.

There was a moment of silence.

Logan continued. "Do you know who...?"

"Not at this time. But if you want to submit a DNA sample, we can check paternity."

He laughed. "Hell no! Like I said, I can't be anywhere near this thing."

"That could be detrimental to your career."

"Damn right it could be. And my marriage." He paused. "I like my marriage. I don't want to lose half of my assets."

"Maybe you should have thought of that before you started fooling around," JD snarked.

Logan's eyes narrowed at him. "Who are you guys, the morality police?"

A silver Mercedes G-Wagon pulled into the driveway.

"Shit!" Logan grumbled. His eyes flicked from the SUV to us. "You're here on a fundraising drive for the department, collecting money for some bullshit charity."

"What charity?" JD asked.

"I don't know. Make something up."

He forced a smile as his wife and two daughters climbed out of the G-Wagon. "Hi, honey!"

Mrs. Shea was an attractive blonde in her early 30s. She gave us a quizzical look.

"Honey, I'd like you to meet Deputies..."

"Wild and Donovan," I said.

JD smiled.

"They're here on a fundraising drive for the department. A youth initiative to give underprivileged kids extracurricular activities and mentorship."

"I think that's a wonderful cause. I'm sure that's something Logan will wholeheartedly support."

He smiled. "Absolutely."

There was an awkward moment.

"Well, thanks for stopping by," Logan said. "Always happy to help the Sheriff's Department."

JD held out his hand, palm up. "We can count on your support."

It took a second to register. "Oh, yeah. Right." Logan dug into his pocket and peeled off a few bills from his money clip. He slapped them into JD's palm.

"Oh, honey. You can give more than that."

He frowned at her but peeled off another couple hundred.

Jack smiled. "Most generous."

She escorted the kids inside.

"We may have further questions," I whispered.

He forced a smile. "Stop by anytime."

He closed the door, and we strolled the walkway to the Porsche. JD's eyes twinkled. "Looks like drinks are on him."

We headed back to the *Avventura*, and I got ready for my evening with Kyra. I didn't figure we'd be dining out, so I hopped on my sport bike and raced up to Pineapple Bay. The wind whistled through my helmet as I hugged the tank. The 1000cc engine howled. Every twist of the throttle was pure adrenaline. Better than any drug.

Kyra greeted me with a warm smile and a steamy embrace. She was staying at the *Mainsail*, a few blocks from the boardwalk. It was another secluded bed-and-breakfast with antique furniture, creaky hardwood floors, and lots of charm.

We ordered lasagna from a great little Italian restaurant, filled our bellies, and washed it down with red wine. It was a nice little evening.

We tumbled around the sheets and wore ourselves out.

It was a little after midnight when Jack called. I was surprised to hear from him. He'd lined up his own entertainment for the evening, and I figured we'd swap stories in the morning. He either had one hell of a story to tell, or something had gone wrong.

29

"Dick Steele OD'd," JD said.

I groaned. "Is he dead?"

"No. EMTs managed to revive him with Narcan. You need to get down here. Remember those girls he met at the *Seven Seas*, Kathy and Megan? Apparently, he was partying with them and broke out the coke. Megan indulged. Kathy didn't. Kathy called 911. Otherwise, Mr. Steele would be in the morgue instead of the hospital."

"Alright, I'm on my way."

"I'll meet you at Coconut General."

I ended the call and filled Kyra in on the situation. "Sorry. Duty calls."

"Go."

"I'll call you tomorrow."

I gave her a last kiss goodbye, got dressed, and headed back to Coconut Key.

The ER was packed. The pale glow of the fluorescents made everyone look ill. By this time of night, people were in as a result of alcohol-related accidents, bar fights, and other maladies.

I called JD as I stepped into the chaos. He was back in a patient room, speaking with Kathy and Megan. I flashed my badge to the security guard and pushed through the double doors. JD gave me directions to the room, and I wandered the hallways as nurses scurried about. I ended the call when I could hear his voice echoing down the hallway as he talked to me.

Megan lay in bed with droopy eyes and an IV running into her arm. Her vitals displayed on the monitor beside the bed. She looked like death warmed over. She'd come pretty close to it.

Her blonde-haired friend, Kathy, sat in a chair talking to JD. The mood was light, having averted disaster.

"Kathy was just giving me the skinny," JD said.

"I'm glad I don't touch the stuff," Kathy said.

Megan said, "I'm never touching it again, that's for sure."

"Where did it come from?" I asked.

"Dick had it," Kathy said.

"You know where he got it from?" I asked.

They both shook their heads.

I asked JD if he had spoken with Mr. Steele yet.

"He wasn't in the mood to talk. But maybe we can give it another try."

"You girls got lucky," I said.

"I promise, no more for me," Megan said.

We left the room and wandered down the hall to find Dick Steele. He was in the same shape as Megan. A little more coherent than the last time JD tried to speak with him. Dick didn't look pleased to see us. "You're not gonna arrest me, are you?"

"Just tell us where you got the drugs," I said.

He hesitated slightly. "Andy."

"Andy Trainor?" I said to clarify.

He nodded.

"When did you buy it from him?"

"A few days ago. I wanted to have some on hand for the new year. I hadn't touched it until today. Then I started partying with the girls, and Megan asked if I had any blow. I figured I might as well break it out. There was still time to get some for New Year's."

"You're lucky to be alive," I said.

"I realize that."

"Where's the coke now?"

He shrugged. "I guess it's at the hotel in the cabana. Don said I could spend the night after the shoot. It was already paid for. He just told me not to trash the place."

"We'll need to get a sworn statement from you that you purchased the drugs from Andy."

"Why?"

"So we can arrest him and charge him with murder and attempted murder."

Dick's eyes rounded.

"He's selling bad stuff," I said.

We took his statement, then left the hospital and headed to the *Seven Seas*.

Carl let us into the cabana, and we searched the area. There was a baggie of cocaine on the coffee table, along with the residue from previous lines. The EMTs and paramedics were more concerned with resuscitating the victims than collecting the evidence. A cleaning crew wouldn't be in until morning. Lucky for us.

We collected the evidence, returned to the station, and logged it. The coke was sent to the lab. We filled out an application for a warrant, then headed back to the marina at *Diver Down*. It was after 2 AM by the time we returned to the *Avventura*. I settled in for the evening.

In the morning, Sheriff Daniels called. "You got your warrant. Go get that son-of-a-bitch!"

I grinned. "With pleasure."

We rounded up a tactical team and gathered outside Andy's door. He lived in *Ceto Court*. It was an upscale building with five floors of luxury apartments with under-building parking and secure entrances. The manager had given us a key, hoping to avoid property damage.

JD pounded a hard fist and shouted, "Coconut County! We have a warrant."

I slid the key into the slot and twisted the handle. The dead-bolt kept the door from budging.

I nodded to Erickson and Faulkner, and they went to work. The battering ram smashed the door, and wood splintered. The door swung wide, and we flooded down the foyer, weapons in the firing position.

So much for the manager's hopes.

ndy had locked himself in the master bathroom. Toilet flushes filtered through the door.

JD kicked it open as Andy tried to flush the better part of a kilo. He hovered over the toilet, breaking chunks off the brick, finally tossing the whole thing in the can, plastic wrap and all.

It didn't go down.

"On the ground!" I shouted. "Now!"

With a bunch of twitchy weapons aimed at him, Andy raised his hands in surrender. He knelt down and ate the tile.

JD advanced and ratcheted the cuffs around his wrists.

We yanked him to his feet, read him his rights, and dragged him from the bathroom.

"Fuck," he groaned. "I knew there was something funny about you two."

We searched the apartment, rummaging through drawers, the closet, coat pockets, the mattress, and air vents.

The place was a slick bachelor pad full of toys and gadgets paid for with excess cash. An 85-inch flatscreen TV in the living room, stylish leather furniture, designer clothes in the closet, an array of expensive shoes, and a collection of watches that was insane.

We found a pound of weed, pills, and a little more cocaine. The lab would analyze everything and tell us more.

Andy was taken to the station, processed, and printed. We filled out after-action reports and paid him a visit. I took a seat across the table from him. Sweat misted his skin, and his nervous eyes flicked between the two of us. There was a mix of fear and anger in his gaze.

"I don't need to tell you that things aren't looking good for you right now. Two people you sold drugs to overdosed last night. It's a miracle they didn't die, or you'd be looking at three counts of murder."

His face crinkled. "I didn't kill anybody."

"You sold cocaine to Tara DeVille that had enough fentanyl in it to kill a small village."

His face crinkled. "No. I didn't."

"You sold the same mix to Dick Steele. Lab results came back. It's exactly the same stuff that killed Tara."

"I don't know what you're talking about. My shit is pure. Why would I want to kill off my customers? I got good customers."

"Had."

His jaw tightened. "You can't pin that on me. What somebody does with something after I sell it to them is their business. I don't know what they mixed it with. People make stupid decisions all the time."

"We're going to test everything we found in your apartment. When we find fentanyl in that mix, you're gonna be in a world of hurt."

His eyes darted between us. The walls were closing in around him, and he knew it. "I didn't sell anybody anything with fentanyl in it."

I didn't buy it for a second. "Start talking about where the stuff is coming from, and maybe you don't spend the rest of your life behind bars."

"Life behind bars or dead on the street. Some choice."

"Nobody forced you to play the game," I said.

He hesitated for a moment, on the verge of tears. "I want a lawyer."

"Suit yourself."

We pushed away from the table, and I banged on the door. A guard buzzed us out a moment later.

"That cat's gonna do serious time," JD said. "At least nobody else is going to die from his stuff."

"Yeah, well, we don't know how much more of that tainted crap is out there. And I sure would like to know where he's getting it."

31

Julian's submarine still hadn't turned up, and neither had Evangeline Everhart. We headed across the island to speak with Julian's friend, Kent Gray. He lived on a 42' sportfish in the *Mangrove Bay* marina.

We strolled the dock, moving past sailboats and motor yachts, looking for the *Dauntless*. We boarded through the transom gate and banged on the salon door.

Kent appeared a moment later, looking uncertain.

I flashed my badge to jog his memory. "We met the other day."

"Yeah, right. You got any leads on who shot Julian? Or do you still think he abducted that girl?"

"I think whoever killed Julian took his submarine. Any idea who that might be?"

"Man, you got me."

"You can't think of any enemies he might have had?"

"Julian could be opinionated and stubborn. Sometimes he rubbed people the wrong way."

"Anybody in particular?"

"Not that I can think of," he said, fidgeting.

"You sure about that?"

"Look, we've all got haters, right? But I don't know anybody pissed off enough to shoot him. What about that girl's brother? I talked to Garrison. He said that guy was considered a suspect."

"Still is, but ballistics didn't match his pistol. So we're looking around for better alternatives."

There was a long moment of silence.

"I wish there was more I could do to help. Julian was a good friend. We all put blood, sweat, and tears into that submarine."

"What was in it for you?"

Kent shrugged. "I don't know. The satisfaction of doing it. The sense of accomplishment. The camaraderie. We were a team. I'm going to miss that."

He frowned.

"Are you sure there's isn't something that you're not telling us?"

"Like what?"

"You tell me."

His eyes flicked between the two of us. "You don't think I had something to do with his death, do you? I mean, what would I have to gain?"

I shrugged.

"I don't know. You and Garrison worked pretty hard on that sub. Maybe you two wanted it for yourselves."

His face crinkled. "That's ridiculous. We could use it anytime we wanted. I told you. Julian was my friend."

"Do you own a gun?"

His brow knitted again. "No." He paused. "Is this like standard operating procedure for you guys? You harass those close to the deceased?"

"Most people are killed by someone they know," I said.

"Have you ever thought that maybe somebody killed him for the submarine?"

"Well, yeah. The thought crossed my mind. That's why I asked you about it."

"I don't think I want to talk to you anymore." He backed away and closed the hatch.

JD and I exchanged a glance, then stepped to the dock.

Jack muttered, "He's hiding something."

"I think you're right about that."

I pulled my phone from my pocket and dialed Isabella. "I need you to check the GPS history of Kent Gray's phone. Let me know if he was anywhere near the marina at the Trident Tower the night of Julian's death."

"I've got a free minute. I'll look it up now." Her fingers clattered against the keyboard. After a minute, she said, "No.

That phone was at the *Salty Dawg* until a little after midnight. Then it found its way back to the *Mangrove Bay* marina and stayed on the boat until the next day at 9 AM."

It was outside the window of opportunity.

"He could have left his phone on the boat, then did his dirty work."

"True. I'll let you figure that out."

"Thanks for the help."

"You got it. I know we're past quid pro quo favors, but I may need some help with the project coming up. I keep threatening to pull you in on something."

I'd been asking a lot of favors from Isabella. It was getting to the point where I owed her again. Or at least, I felt like it. "Let me know what you need and when you need it."

I was trying to avoid contract work. It was often a gray area that I didn't much care for.

"I say we go look for that sub," JD suggested after I ended the call.

"That's like looking for a needle in a haystack."

"What else have we got to do?" He grinned. "You never know what we might find."

We hopped into the Porsche and drove back to *Diver Down*. We grabbed lunch at the bar, then returned to the *Avventura*.

Almost all of our gear had been stolen during one of our expeditions. While we were diving, pirates had raided the boat and absconded with quite a few of JD's expensive toys, including his sonar drone. That gave him an excuse to upgrade to the latest model.

My eye was drawn to someone strutting down the dock toward the *Avventura*. Someone I didn't expect to see.

"Aren't you supposed to stay out of Coconut Key?" I asked Kyra as she crossed the passerelle to join us on the aft deck.

She smirked. "You know me. I don't always do what I'm told. Besides, I didn't want to leave town without saying goodbye."

I lifted a curious eyebrow.

"Change of plans. I'm leaving a day early. I figured it's probably best to get out of town, so I loaded up a few things and packed my car. I'm gonna take a leisurely drive, and I'll be in Houston just in time to move into my new place."

My stomach tightened a little. I hated to see her go. "It's probably for the best. It's dangerous for you around here."

"Danger is the spice of life, isn't it?"

"I think you might need psychological counseling," I teased.

She laughed. "I thought we'd already established that."

I smiled at her.

"Well, I'm terrible at goodbyes. So let's just say until next time."

"Until next time."

She gave me a long, tight hug. Her warm body radiated.

"I'll walk you to your car," I said when our bodies parted.

We left the boat and strolled the dock toward the parking lot.

"It probably wasn't too smart to come back here," I said.

She shrugged. "They're looking for me in Pineapple Bay now. Plus, some things are worth the risk." She looked up at me with her smoldering eyes, her lashes fluttering.

I tried to drag the walk to the car out as long as possible. I knew this was probably the last time I'd see her for a while. Still, we reached the car way too soon.

"It's been fun, deputy."

"I agree, special agent."

We stared at each other for a long, awkward moment.

"I don't do the long-distance thing. It never works out. And I can't imagine you're a big fan of it either." She lifted on her toes and planted her pillowy lips against mine.

I tasted her lip gloss and inhaled her fruity shampoo for the last time. We drew the kiss out for as long as possible. It was nice. Full of passion. My heart thumped. Blood coursed through my veins.

She broke free, and we caught our breath.

"I'll call you when I get settled."

"Have a safe trip. Watch your back."

"I will. Take care of yourself," she said.

I smiled and watched her get into her car. She twisted the ignition, pulled out of the parking space, and rolled onto the road.

I couldn't help but feel a little hollow.

I returned to the *Avventura* and tried to clear my head.

"I was just starting to like her, too," JD said.

"Yeah. I know the feeling."

I disconnected shore power and water and cast off the lines. JD took the helm and idled us out of the marina.

The troubles and disappointments faded with the waves. The sea had a way of calming the mind. At least on a day like this.

The superyacht plowed through the teal swells, heading toward where we found Julian floating in the water. It was hard to say how far he had drifted. He could have been dumped nearby or miles away.

Our excursion would be an afternoon on the water and an adventure.

We were always down for both.

32

We dropped anchor and readied the dive gear, just in case. The boat pitched and rolled with the swells. The sun hung high overhead, sparkling the water, and a gentle breeze drifted across the boat.

JD grabbed the heavy case that housed the drone and lugged it to the aft deck. He flipped the latches and opened the case lined with custom-cut foam. He removed the state-of-the-art drone that looked like a Tomahawk missile with a propeller on one end.

The wireless device connected to a phone or tablet. A floating surface buoy allowed it to maintain a wireless connection, even when out of range. It would switch over to the 5G network. You could program in a search grid, and the remote device would sweep the area, providing a 3D image of the seafloor. It was impressive technology, and I'm sure the damn thing cost more than the Porsche.

We launched the drone from the swim platform, and the sleek gray device plunged into the water. JD sat on the aft deck and tapped on his iPad, punching in the details of its mission.

We'd used something similar in our search for the lost treasure of Jacques De La Fontaine, which we still hadn't found. Discovering the wreckage of the *Royal Revenge* had scratched our treasure-hunting itch for the time being. Demi De Luca was still salvaging items, and artifacts were being restored to their former glory.

With any luck, we'd be able to add the sunken submarine to our list of discoveries.

I grabbed a couple of ice-cold beers from the fridge, twisted the tops with a hiss, and handed a long neck to JD. We clinked the amber bottles.

"To deep sea adventures," JD said with a grin.

We spent the rest of the afternoon lounging on the aft deck, drinking beer, and relaxing. We were technically working, but not really.

The drone made a couple sweeps, but nothing turned up.

Jack programmed in new coordinates and sent the thing off on another mission.

"What do you think is really going on here?" JD asked.

I shrugged. "I have a few ideas."

"It's a lot of trouble to build a submarine," JD said.

"Sometimes you do a thing not because it's easy, but because it is hard."

"Garrison had a point. The cartel would pay big money for a submarine capable of transporting drugs from Latin America undetected."

"You think that's why he built it?"

JD shrugged. "It might have been a consideration."

"Julian had no priors. No history of drug involvement. Seems like an abrupt change of direction. A big risk to take. And his wife is loaded. He didn't need money."

"Maybe he knew it was going south, and she was planning on divorcing him."

I shook my head. "He'd walk away with a sizable chunk of assets. I don't think running drugs was his motivation to build that submarine. Julian was a fanatic, from what I gather. He was obsessed."

The sun dipped down over the horizon, and we watched the sky transform into multiple shades of pink, orange, and purple.

We decided to shut down the operation for the day and collect the drone. JD piloted it back to the stern, and we collected the device, toweled it off, and stored it snug in its case. JD lugged it back inside, and I weighed anchor. By the time we got back to the marina, we were both ready for dinner.

We stopped in *Diver Down* and took a seat at the bar. Teagan greeted us with a smile and a glass of whiskey. She asked about our day, and we caught her up to speed.

"Got any vibe on where that sub might be?" JD asked.

Teagan's supposed psychic powers came and went. She didn't like to use her gift. She thought of it as a curse. Felt like there was always a heavy price to pay. I didn't know what to think about the whole thing, but she had a hell of an intuition. And when she gambled, she was the luckiest person on the planet.

She placated JD by pretending to tune into the sub's location. "I can see it now," she said in a dramatic tone.

JD gave her a doubtful glance.

"It somewhere... somewhere... underwater!"

Jack frowned.

She stuck her tongue out at him.

"I'm telling you, harness that power, and you could solve crimes."

"Sorry. That's not how it works."

Denise called as we were finishing our first round. "Hey, the lab was able to pull a partial print from the baggie of cocaine you recovered from the cabana at the *Seven Seas*. Guess who matched besides Dick Steele?"

33

"Billy Diamond and Tara DeVille," Denise said.

That hung there for a moment.

"What were Billy Diamond's prints doing on Dick's baggie?"

"I don't know. But it's a good thing Billy had a previous record and was in the system. Same with Tara DeVille."

"Nice work."

"Thank you," she said in a cheery tone.

I ended the call and updated Jack. We thought about the situation and tried to piece everything together. I had a theory developing, and I figured I could sort it out by talking to Billy Diamond.

"Are you thinking what I'm thinking?" JD asked.

I nodded.

We chowed down on dinner, then decided to pay a casual off-duty visit to Mr. Diamond. We caught up with him at a new venue called *Verse*. It was a small club where Coconut Key's burgeoning rap scene was happening.

There was a small stage and a tower of speakers on either side. A DJ would play the backing tracks, and wannabe rappers would prance around the stage, spitting lyrics into the microphone, getting the crowd amped up.

Heavy kick drums and booming bass rumbled from the speakers, vibrating my chest as we entered the club.

The place was packed.

There were plenty of short skirts and painted-on dresses. Long legs and stiletto heels. Pert, jiggling assets. There were quite a few gangsters in the audience—some wannabes, some the real deal. A lot of gang tattoos. It could be a tough club at times on the edge of Jamaica Village. Not the greatest neighborhood in town.

Billy Diamond liked to think of himself as a thug, but he was anything but. He had prior's for possession and DUI, but nothing violent. He wasn't slinging dope on a street corner or doing drive-by shootings. Hell, according to his record, he had graduated with honors from the Coconut Key high school and had attended Vanden for a semester, majoring in finance.

Billy pranced around on the stage, trying to look hard, screaming tough lyrics into the microphone. It wasn't half bad, and he got the crowd pretty riled up.

We ordered a drink from the bar and hung out at the back of the club for most of the show.

Billy finished his last song and thanked the audience. We headed to the side of the stage and confronted him as he stepped off, sweaty and out of breath.

I flashed my badge again and shouted, "Hey Billy, we just have a few questions for you."

His nervous eyes flicked between the two of us.

It was a tiny club that didn't have a green room for stage acts.

We found a booth at the back of the club and had a conversation before the next act took the stage.

"You're aware that Dick Steele OD'd, aren't you?"

"Yeah, I heard something about that."

"It was the same stuff that killed Tara."

He looked more frightened than surprised. Somehow, he already knew.

I continued, "Your fingerprints were on the baggie of drugs."

He swallowed hard and said nothing.

"You want to tell me how your fingerprints got there?"

He shrugged. "How should I know?"

"You know what I think?"

He shifted uncomfortably.

"I think you got tired of Dick Steele giving the stiff one to your girlfriend. I think you mixed up a cocktail of bad drugs, and I think you replaced his stash with your bad batch."

He didn't say anything for a moment, but guilt was written all over his face. "What are you talking about?"

"It would have been easy for you to do. Slip it into a pocket on set while he's off diddling your girlfriend on camera. Except you didn't count on one thing. You didn't count on Tara going through his pockets, finding his coke, and doing a line or two for herself."

His face tensed, and his cheeks reddened. He twitched slightly. "That's bullshit. And you can't prove any of it."

"Oh, I think we can put together a pretty good circumstantial case."

"I'm done talking to you two." He slipped out of the booth and hustled through the crowd, looking back over his shoulder to see if we were following him.

His prints on the baggie probably weren't enough for a warrant, but we would try to get one in the morning.

In law enforcement, there is what you know, and what you can prove. I knew Billy had tried to kill Dick Steele. But I didn't know if I could prove it.

34

It was around 4 AM when my phone buzzed the nightstand. I was out cold, and it took several rings to convince me to leave dreamland. I reached a sleepy hand for the phone, glanced at the caller ID, then swiped the screen.

The sheriff's gruff voice filtered through the speaker. "I need you two nitwits to get over to the Delphine."

"What happened now?" I scratched.

"Several neighbors reported hearing gunshots in unit #322. Deputies did a welfare check and... Well, you'll see when you get there."

"We are on our way."

I dragged myself out of bed, got dressed, and descended the steps to the main deck. I banged on the hatch to JD's VIP stateroom.

He groaned.

I relayed the information, and before too long, he emerged, bleary-eyed, with tousled hair.

We pulled ourselves together and headed to the *Delphine*. It was an upscale apartment complex with five stories and gated under-building parking.

Lights flickered from patrol units. An ambulance in the parking lot flashed red and whites.

Somebody had propped open the lobby door. We stepped inside and took the elevator up to the third floor.

Camera flashes spilled out of the apartment, and deputies crowded the hallway as forensic investigators evaluated the scene.

A few curious neighbors gawked in the corridor.

The tinny, metallic scent of blood lingered in the air as we stepped into the apartment.

Billy's body lay slumped on the white leather sofa. He had redecorated the walls with his brains. Crimson sludge splattered the cheap painting that hung on the wall above the couch. A black 9mm pistol lay on the hardwoods not far away.

It was a nice apartment. Large flatscreen display, bumping stereo system, a balcony with a decent view. There was a guitar in one corner and a mountain bike in another. Sad emo music pumped through speakers—the kind of songs you listen to when you lose your girlfriend, then do a lot of drugs to cope. The kind of band with a singer that would be dead by 27.

Brenda examined the remains, wearing pink nitrile gloves.

The first thing I looked for was blood spatter on Billy's right hand—blowback from when he put the pistol to his head and pulled the trigger. I get concerned if I don't see it in these types of cases. The case appeared to be pretty cut and dry, but you never knew around here.

"I think he was feeling guilty about Tara's death," JD said. "He tried to eliminate a rival and eliminated the object of his desire instead."

"I think you're right." I frowned and shook my head. It was senseless.

"Judging by the body temperature, he's been dead for about an hour," Brenda said. "That would be consistent with the reports of neighbors hearing a gunshot."

Forensic investigators collected the pistol. After the scene was documented, Brenda and her team bagged the body, and we searched the apartment. We found a little bit of cocaine, some weed, and a few pills. I was anxious to see what the lab would have to say about them.

By the time Billy's body was wheeled out on a gurney, Paris Delaney and her news crew were in the hallway capturing footage.

We interviewed some of the neighbors, and everyone pretty much had the same story. They all recalled hearing the gunshot around the same time. No one had seen anyone coming or going.

Paris confronted me as we walked the hallway toward the elevator, the camera hovering near my face.

"What can you tell us about the incident?"

I tried to play nice, even though I was a little irritated with her. "We have a deceased male, dead from an apparent self-inflicted gunshot."

"Can you confirm the deceased is, in fact, Billy Diamond?"

"We're withholding the name, pending notification of next of kin."

"Billy Diamond was dating Tara DeVille. He was present the day she died on your boat."

My eyes narrowed at her. "I have no further comment."

We continued toward the elevator, and the camera crew followed. I pressed the call button, and it lit up. I couldn't get away from her fast enough.

"Is there a connection here?"

I didn't answer.

"Are you considering Tara's death a homicide?"

The elevator doors slid open, and JD and I stepped aboard. I pressed the *door-close* button as fast as I could.

Paris blocked it with her hand, and she hustled in with her crew.

It was cramped, especially with the camera and the spotlight shining on me.

"What's the connection between Dick Steele's OD and Tara's death? Was that an attempted murder? Did Billy Diamond have any involvement?"

I kept my eyes forward and ignored her.

The doors opened on the first floor, and we stepped out and hustled through the lobby.

Paris and her crew followed, asking more questions.

We climbed into the Porsche, and JD fired up the engine.

Paris was angling to make this story as dramatic as possible, still trying to imply some inappropriate behavior on our part. Her crew grabbed footage of us leaving the *Delphine* in Jack's Porsche. That would only contribute to the intrigue.

"Sometimes that girl can really get under my skin," JD said.

I couldn't disagree.

We headed back to the marina at *Diver Down* and tried to grab a little shut-eye. I was a little amped up and irritated, so it took a while to nod off.

It wasn't long before the morning sun crept through the cracks in the blinds. I slept till about 9 AM, then pulled myself out of bed. I showered, dressed, then grilled breakfast in the galley.

JD joined me on the aft deck, and we chowed down on crispy bacon and ham and cheese omelets. We washed it down with fresh coffee. The sun sparkled on the water, and the amber rays bathed boats in a warm glow. The day felt optimistic.

"What do you say we go sub hunting today?"

35

I took Buddy out for a walk, then we prepped the gear, disconnected shore power and water, and cast off the lines.

Before long, we were out on the open water, enjoying the cool breeze and the amber rays.

We picked a location and launched the sonar drone, then relaxed on the aft deck, fishing while the remote device scoured the seafloor.

We spent the morning chasing a ghost and came up with nothing. We didn't catch any fish either.

Jack took the helm, and I weighed anchor. We headed back to the marina and grabbed lunch at *Diver Down*. I didn't think we'd be able to expense the boat fuel back to the county, but JD would try.

I didn't figure we'd get much accomplished today. It was New Year's Eve, and we had the party scheduled for tonight. Jack had hired a catering crew, and after lunch, we started prepping the boat for the event. We cleaned up the salon, the galley, and tidied up the guest staterooms. I knew we would have a few overnight guests. I was cleaning out the room Tara DeVille had used when I spotted a little baggie in between the bunk and the nightstand. Forensic investigators must have missed it. There was a little cocaine residue in the bag.

I snapped on a pair of nitrile gloves, put it into an evidence bag, labeled it, and took it down to the station. I asked the lab to do superglue fuming to pull prints from the plastic. I was sure I wouldn't hear back for a few days due to the long weekend.

It was a rare occasion when JD wore a tuxedo, and when he did, he did it with flair. The black coat with tails, and the silver silk vest with a brocade pattern, made him look regal. His hair was pulled back into a slick ponytail.

I wore a *DiFiore* tux, and JD sprang for outfits for the band. The last time the guys in *Wild Fury* had worn tuxedos was their high school prom.

The boat was stocked with beer, liquor, and wine. The catering crew arrived and began preparing for the guests.

Dizzy, Crash, and Styxx showed up, looking respectable. They were a little uncomfortable with tight collars and formal shoes.

JD lifted an impressed brow.

"Let's get this party started," Crash said with a smile.

"Just don't go overboard until after the set," I cautioned.

Wild Fury was scheduled to play from 10 PM till 11:30 PM. We invited the neighbors to minimize noise complaints, but I didn't think we'd have much of an issue tonight. It would be a small, intimate gathering of friends and top-tier fans. The marina was filled with revelers.

It wasn't long before guests began arriving—girls in slinky evening wear with plunging necklines, shimmering sequins, and long legs. Plenty of updos and sparkling earrings.

We welcomed the guests aboard, and the waitstaff mingled with trays of hors d'oeuvres and glasses of champagne.

Sheriff Daniels showed up, looking stylish. But the real showstopper was Denise. I had to pick my tongue up and put it back in my mouth.

36

The black sequined dress hugged her sumptuous form like a second skin. The deep V-neck created anticipation of a wardrobe malfunction, her all-natural endowments jiggling, unrestrained. A slit at the front of the dress ran all the way up her thigh, stopping just short of the promised land. She wore gold, strappy heels and gold hoop earrings. Her emerald eyes sparkled, and her smooth, creamy skin glowed. Her shimmery red hair cascaded down her shoulders. She was hotter than a dragon's breath.

I couldn't breathe.

JD stopped her as she crossed the gangway. "I'm sorry, but you can't come aboard."

Her eyes narrowed at him. "Why not?"

"I specifically said dress to impress. This is not impressive."

She gave him a sassy look. "Really?"

"This is downright lethal." JD pointed at me. "He's feeling short of breath, and I'm having heart palpitations."

She smirked. "Want me to call an ambulance?"

"You might have to."

"Stop harassing your coworker," Daniels said.

"All in good fun," JD replied.

"You look quite striking, deputy," Daniels said to her.

"You're looking pretty snazzy yourself, sheriff."

He tried to hide a grin.

"Can I offer you a drink?" JD asked. "A glass of wine? Perhaps the bubbly stuff?"

"It's New Year's Eve. A glass of champagne sounds nice."

JD flagged down a waiter. He zipped through the crowd and delivered the sparkling delight. Denise took the flute with her elegant fingers, and JD lifted his glass to toast. "To a new year filled with health, wealth, and joy."

We all clinked glasses and sipped our beverages.

Denise drew plenty of eyes. There was nothing unusual about that. She managed to make the uniform look pretty damn good, but this was next level. Her makeup was flaw-less, and her eyes smoldered with smoky shadow. Her lips glimmered with gloss, staining the rim of the champagne flute.

"Don't get any funny ideas," Daniels muttered in my ear, noticing my incessant gaze. Denise had a magnetic quality, and I couldn't seem to peel my eyes away.

Daniels had a policy against interoffice romances. In the current climate, that could lead to all kinds of trouble and open the department up to liability. It's all fine and dandy when it goes well, but breakups can be nasty.

Apart from that, he looked at Denise like a daughter. We all felt protective of her.

More guests arrived, and pretty soon, the boat was packed. People mixed and mingled, and champagne flowed. It was pretty tame for a *Wild Fury* party. At least at the beginning. People kept their clothes on, which was a rarity around here.

The band went on at 10 PM and played an acoustic set on the aft deck. Softer versions of their classics drifted through the boat.

The band finished their set and played a few encores.

As midnight approached, people crowded on the sky deck to watch the fireworks.

The hour drew near, and the countdown started.

10...

Nine...

Eight...

Denise mingled through the crowd and found me. "There you are. I've been looking for you. Happy New Year, Tyson!"

Three...

Two...

One...

"Happy New Year, Denise."

People in party hats blew their horns. Confetti was tossed into the air. People hugged and kissed.

Denise flung her arms around me, lifted on her tiptoes, and planted one on my lips. It started as a friendly peck, then grew into something much deeper.

Fireworks lit up the sky, popping and crackling. Explosions in multiple colors. Thunderous booms echoed in the night. The water glittered with the reflection of the glowing displays launched from barges on the water.

There were certainly fireworks between us.

Rules were meant to be broken, weren't they?

She pulled away just as I had the urge to pull her close. She looked at me with guilty green eyes. "Whoops!"

There was an awkward moment between us, and from the corner of my eye, I saw Daniels glaring at me.

Denise smirked and sauntered away, weaving through the crowd, a little tipsy.

I looked at Daniels and shrugged innocently.

He marched toward me.

"She kissed me," I defended.

"I told you not to mess around with that girl's head. She's not one of your casual flings."

"I know."

"She's the real deal. You two get more ass than a toilet seat, and I don't see that changing anytime soon. I don't want you breaking that girl's heart. If you're going to go there, you'd better put a ring on it."

"I'm not gonna mess with her head."

People sang for Auld Lang Syne, the new year upon us.

My heart still thudded, and my mind raced.

After the fireworks, the crowd started to thin, and the hard-core partiers remained. In typical *Wild Fury* fashion, dresses hit the deck, and the Jacuzzi saw some lewd activity.

The party raged into the wee hours of the morning. I looked around the boat for Denise but couldn't find her. I figured she had slipped away amid the chaos.

The guys in the band had paired up with some eager attendees, and the last time I saw Jack, he was talking to a lovely brunette.

I was ready to call it a night and get out of the suit. I made my way to my stateroom and noticed a pair of gold heels on the deck next to a black sequined dress.

Denise was in my bed, passed out.

37

"**O**h, shit!" Denise said in the morning, realizing where she was.

Amber rays of sun pierced the blinds. The boat was still after the adventurous night.

Denise clutched the covers over her naked form, trying to replay the events of the evening. "Oh, my god! We didn't... did we?"

She cringed.

I'm not going to lie—I enjoyed watching her squirm. I thought about messing with her, but I figured I'd put her mind at ease. "No. You'd remember if we did."

She rolled her eyes.

"You pretty much threw yourself at me last night," I teased.

"Shut up. I did not."

"You don't remember kissing me on the sky deck?"

"What!? In your dreams."

I raised my hands innocently. "Ask Daniels."

Her emerald eyes narrowed at me, trying to discern the truth. "How did I get in here, and who took my dress off?"

"You were in bed, and your dress was on the floor when I got here."

"And nothing happened?"

"You were passed out. I wasn't going to take advantage of you. But you were clearly looking to get frisky."

"I was tired. This was convenient."

"Right..." I snarked.

"Would you turn around and close your eyes so I can get dressed?"

"Seen one, you've seen them all."

"You haven't seen this."

I smirked, then complied, rolling over. I was a perfect gentleman. I didn't peek, and I didn't even look under the covers the night before. But I had to admit, the thought of Denise naked in my stateroom did arouse certain desires.

She shimmied into the sequined dress, pulled the straps over her shoulders, and grabbed her stilettos from the deck.

"Okay, you can look now."

I rolled back over. She looked just as delicious in the morning as she did the night before. A little more tousled, but I wasn't complaining. "Do you want breakfast?"

"Hell, no. I'm sneaking out of here before anyone sees me."

"Nothing happened."

"No one's ever going to believe that." She stepped to the sliding glass door and pulled it open.

"You want me to give you a ride?"

"No. I'll catch a cab."

"Goodbye, Denise," I taunted.

"Goodbye, Tyson," she replied in kind.

She slipped out and plunged down the molded steps to the aft deck. The patter of her feet across the passerelle filtered through the air.

I chuckled, pulled myself out of bed, and took a shower.

In the galley, I put on a pot of coffee and started grilling up breakfast. The place was silent. Not a creature was stirring. The boat was a mess, lined with empty beer bottles, wine glasses, champagne flutes, and debris.

Jack didn't surface, so I ended up eating breakfast on the sky deck alone, taking in the dawn of the new year.

I took Buddy out for a run. The island was like a ghost town. Everyone was too hungover to move.

Jack was up by the time I got back to the boat, having breakfast with the brunette from last night.

We spent a leisurely day watching bowl games, cleaning up, and indulging in a little hair of the dog.

The next day, trouble started when Denise called. "Hey, we got a call at the station from Clara Cook. Isn't that one of your suspects wives?"

"Garrison Cook's wife? I didn't know he was married."

"She said some guy showed up at the marina, threatening her. Daniels wants you to see if there's any connection to Julian's murder."

"We are on it." I teased her. "By the way, you left your panties here."

"They're not mine. I wasn't wearing any."

If she was trying to get a rise out of me, she was successful.

She ended the call, and we drove to *Pirates' Cove*. We found Garrison's sailboat, and I banged on the transom. I figured Clara might be a little skittish since someone had threatened her. To disarm her, I shouted, "Coconut County!"

The hatch opened, and Clara poked her head out of the cabin. She was an attractive woman in her early 30s with medium-length chocolate brown hair and caramel eyes. She had full lips and olive skin.

I flashed my badge, and she looked relieved. "Please, come aboard."

We stepped into the cockpit and descended the ladder into the cabin. She cradled a newborn, who just started to cry with the commotion. She calmed him with a comforting voice, bouncing him in her arms slightly.

"I understand you were threatened?"

"This guy came around looking for Garrison. I told him he wasn't here. He asked when he'd be back, and I said I didn't know. He just had this unsettling demeanor about him, and these cold eyes. Gave me a chill just looking at him. He said, *tell Garrison he'd better start cooperating. I'm getting tired of games. He's got such a nice family, a nice boat, a great life. I'd hate for anything to happen to that.* That's a threat, right?"

"It wouldn't make me feel warm and fuzzy."

"I told him I had a gun and that he needed to leave."

"Do you have a gun?"

"No."

"What about Garrison?"

"I made him get rid of all the guns. I don't want them around here. And as much as I love living on the sailboat, I told him we need to get a house. I want Timmy to have a yard. It's okay now while he's not walking around, but I think once he gets mobile, I'll be a nervous wreck with him on this boat."

"Have you ever seen this guy before?"

She shook her head.

"What did he look like?"

"He had sandy-blond hair. A short, scraggly beard. He was maybe 6'1". Athletic build. Brown eyes."

"Did he mention a name?"

"No."

"Do you have any surveillance cameras on the boat?"

"No, but I think we should."

"I'll check with the neighbors and the office."

"If you find him, can you arrest him? I mean, you can't go around threatening people."

"These kinds of situations are really difficult to prosecute. Until he's done something or made the threat in writing, there's not much we can do."

"Julian's death has me really spooked. I'm wondering what Julian got himself into. Now it seems like Garrison is dragged into it."

"Where is Garrison now?"

"He's out running errands, and he's supposed to be picking me up something from the store."

"What do you think Julian may have been involved in?"

"I don't know."

"Drugs?"

"I'm beginning to wonder," she said. "What did this guy mean *if Garrison doesn't cooperate?*"

"Do you know what they planned on doing with the submarine?"

"I know that Julian wanted to cross the ocean in it. I thought he was crazy, and I told Garrison absolutely not. I didn't even like them tooling around here in it. Anything can go wrong with one of those things. And nobody's coming to save you when you're 100 feet under the water."

"Garrison never said anything to you about any illegal activity?"

"No. And if he had, I'd have given him an earful, and his ass would be out on the street. He's got responsibilities now. He needs to start acting like it."

"Have you talked to Garrison about this?"

She hesitated for a moment, and her face tightened.

"Is there something you're not telling me?"

She sighed and said, "Okay, this wasn't the first time this guy came by looking for him. I called Garrison before I called you. I told him about the situation, and he said he'd handle it. I'm sorry, but that answer is not acceptable to me. I don't like people coming around my home threatening me. This isn't a game. I don't know what he's into, but it's got to stop."

Someone boarded the boat. Footsteps clattered across the deck, and the hatch opened.

38

Brilliant rays of Florida sunshine spilled into the cabin, backlighting Garrison as he climbed in. He looked at us with confusion. "What's going on here?"

Clara laid into him. "Some guy came by the boat and threatened me. That's what's going on. And you won't do anything about it! How about you tell me what's really going on?"

Garrison's face tightened.

JD and I sat back and prepared to watch the fireworks.

"It's nothing. I owe the guy a little money. It's no big deal. He's just acting tough."

"How much money?" Clara asked.

"A couple thousand dollars. It's nothing."

"What do you owe him money for? Does this have anything to do with Julian?"

"No. Would you just calm down?"

That was the wrong thing to say.

Clara's face reddened, and she looked like she was about to explode. The veins in her neck bulged, and her eyes protruded. "Calm down!? You want me to calm down? Someone threatened our family, Garrison."

"Can we discuss this in private?" he asked. Garrison looked at us. "I'm sorry for the trouble. She shouldn't have called you. It's really not a big deal."

Clara growled at him.

"What's this gentleman's name?" I asked.

Garrison hesitated a moment. "Jesse. I don't know his last name."

"Why do you owe him money?" Clara asked.

Garrison stammered, "He provided some parts for the submarine."

"That sounds like it's Julian's problem."

"Well, I ordered the parts from him. Since Julian isn't around anymore, I'm on the hook for it."

"Does he work in a parts store for submarines?" I asked, trying not to sound too snarky.

"We met at one of the DIY groups. He's got a connection and can get parts cheaper than I can find them."

"Do you have his contact information?"

Garrison froze. "Look, if you harass him, it's just gonna make things worse for me. I'll settle up with him today, and this will be done."

"Where are you going to get a couple thousand dollars?" Clara asked. "We've barely got enough in the account to cover the slip fees, groceries, baby formula, and insurance."

"Honey, these gentlemen don't want to hear about all of our problems."

She growled again.

Garrison addressed us. "Again, I'm sorry for the trouble. I'll get this sorted out. I promise."

"I'm beginning to think maybe this guy had something to do with Julian's death," I said.

Garrison stared at me for a long moment. "I can give you the number I have for him if you want to talk to him."

"Yeah, that would be great. You know where he lives?"

"I don't."

"Did he ever threaten Julian?"

"I don't know."

"Why didn't you mention this before?" I asked.

"I didn't put it all together. I mean, I'm the only one who dealt with him. Julian had me in charge of acquisitions. He handled the design and implementation."

Something odd was going on here.

"If he shows up again, call me immediately," I said.

We left the boat, and I called Isabella. I gave her Jesse's phone number. "Can you give me the GPS history on that phone?"

Her fingers tapped the keyboard. "Looks like a prepaid cellular."

"Was it at the marina at the *Trident Towers* the night of Julian's death?"

Her fingers danced across the keys. "Off the grid."

"Where is it now?"

"Off the grid."

My face tightened with frustration.

"Can you associate that phone with a residential address?"

"It shows up all over town a couple times a day. But it looks like he's smart enough to never use it from his home address. I'll let you know if it pops up on the grid."

I thanked her for her time, then dialed Denise. "Hey, I need you to search arrest records for males, late 20s to early 30s, by the name of Jesse." I gave her a description of the guy.

"I'll see what I can find."

"Thank you," I said before ending the call.

"I think we need to have a word with Kent Gray," JD said.

"I agree."

I figured he might have a little insight into the situation.

We climbed into the Porsche and headed over to *Mangrove Bay*. We found his sportfishing boat, and I banged on the transom.

He didn't answer.

We stepped into the cockpit, and I banged on the hatch, then peered in through the tinted windows.

He could have been hiding below deck, but I didn't hear a sound.

I called Isabella and asked her to track Kent's phone. She told me it was sitting at the *Salty Dawg*. I should have just had her track the device originally and saved us a trip. I was always careful with my favors from her. I didn't want to go overboard, even though I was already well over.

We drove to the little hole-in-the-wall bar. The place was dim and smelled like beer, whiskey, and bleach. There was a small stage, a jukebox, and rows of booths and tables. Regulars sat at the bar and drank themselves into oblivion.

It wasn't very crowded this time of day. There were a few old timers, and a stringy blonde with stork legs, cut-off jeans, and a muffin top. She was quite the catch for this place.

Kent sat at the bar with a half-empty glass of whiskey in front of him. Judging by his bloodshot, glassy eyes, this wasn't his first drink of the day. He looked a little disheveled.

JD leaned against the bar on one side, and I flanked Kent on the other. Our presence was claustrophobic.

"How's it going, Kent?" I asked.

"It's going," he replied.

"We just have a few additional questions for you."

"Ask away. I'm an open book."

That wasn't exactly the case.

"Tell me about Jesse," I said.

His face stiffened. "I don't know anybody named Jesse."

He was lying.

He fidgeted and averted his gaze. His foot bounced incessantly, and he took another sip of his whiskey.

"You shouldn't lie to us, Kent. That's gonna put us on bad terms. You don't want to be on bad terms, do you?"

"I don't know anybody named Jesse."

"He's the guy that threatened Garrison's wife."

Kent swallowed hard.

I continued. "Garrison says he owes him money, and that he supplied parts for the submarine."

"Garrison does a lot of business with shady people."

"You sure you don't know the guy?"

"No." His eyes flicked away, and he gave a nervous glance around.

I flagged the bartender down and slapped a few bills on the counter. "Another round for my friend."

The bartender scooped up the money, grabbed a bottle from the well, spun it around, and filled Kent's glass.

"Kent, you need to start telling us the truth. Your friend is dead. Your other friend's family is in jeopardy. For all I know, you've been threatened. Maybe that's why you're reluctant to talk. Let us help you."

Kent hesitated. He glanced around again.

"Something's got you pretty spooked," I said. "What is it?"

"Not here," he muttered.

We left the bar and found a secluded booth in the back.

39

"Look, Jesse just showed up out of nowhere," Kent said in a hushed tone. He took another sip of his whiskey. "He started making demands. At first, he offered money, but we weren't interested. Then he started making threats."

"What did he want?" I asked.

"He wanted Julian to take the sub to Colombia, pick up a load of cocaine, and bring it back. He said he had a connection here to move the product, and we could all make a ton of money. Jesse said if we didn't cooperate, there would be consequences."

"Did he kill Julian?" I asked.

"That's what I thought at first." Kent gave another nervous glance around the bar. "Look, I didn't have anything to do with this. You have to believe me."

"I'm listening."

"I don't know where to start."

"Start at the beginning."

"Garrison has the submarine."

That hung in the air for a moment.

"Where is it?"

Kent hesitated. "I don't know."

"Did Garrison kill Julian?"

"He went out with him on the sub that night. Julian turns up dead, and Garrison has the sub. Doesn't take a rocket scientist to figure out what went down."

"Why would he kill Julian?"

"He thought Julian was gonna fuck everything up."

"Everything?"

Kent gave another worried glance around, then surveyed us for a moment. "Can I trust you two?"

"More so than any of your so-called friends," I said.

He seemed to agree with that sentiment. In a subtle but enthused tone, he said, "We found it."

His eyes sparkled a little.

"Found what?"

"The HMS Silverstone."

I exchanged a curious glance with Jack. We didn't know what he was talking about.

Kent looked at us with disbelief. "You've never heard of the Silverstone?"

"Refresh my memory."

"During World War II, banks were moving gold out of Europe, fearing it would be confiscated by the Germans during an invasion. We're talking thousands of metric tons of gold bullion. Most of it was carried on merchant ships, taken across the Atlantic to banks in New York and elsewhere. There were shipments going all over the world to different ports. France, Norway, England—they were all trying to safeguard their gold. The Silverstone was heading to a reserve bank in Texas."

I gave him a doubtful glance. "What does this have to do with anything?"

"The Caribbean and the Gulf were swarming with U-boats. They were taking out merchant ships at will. Most people don't realize how close to home the war came. Anyway, the Silverstone went down, followed by an oil tanker. They're less than a mile apart on the ocean floor."

"And you planned to recover the gold from the Silverstone."

He nodded. "But we ran into a slight issue. The tanker has a hold full of 90,000 gallons of oil. Every year that ship is down there, the more it corrodes. It's a ticking time bomb. The coast could be devastated by a massive leak. It would take years to clean up. We found both shipwrecks. Julian wanted to contact the Office of Response and Restoration so they could start the process of reclaiming the oil from the wreckage before it leaked into the ocean."

"That sounds like a good idea," I said.

"Garrison got worried that the cleanup crew might find the Silverstone. Word would get out, and our find would become public knowledge."

"And you wanted the gold for yourselves?"

"The current value is $11 billion," Kent said.

That drifted across the table and hung like mist.

JD and I exchanged an impressed glance.

"That seems like more than enough to go around," I said.

"For the three of us, yeah. But there are all kinds of legal issues and finders fees. Britain will most likely make a claim on the money, even though it was a merchant ship and not a military vessel. I don't know. I'm not an expert in maritime law."

"So you were gonna bring up the gold and sell it on the black market?"

"We were going to recover it, then figure out what to do with it," he said, trying to sound innocent.

"So, Garrison shot Julian and took the sub."

"I didn't see it with my own eyes, but he implied that he did and said I'd meet the same fate if I gave him any trouble."

"Sounds like a good friend."

"While all that was going down, Jesse kept harassing us to work with him. As you can imagine, what he was offering was not nearly as lucrative as $11 billion. And as much as I'm passionate about that submarine, I'm not too keen on taking it to Colombia and back. It would require at least two people to man that thing for a journey like that."

"Where is the wreckage of the Silverstone?" JD asked with more than a hint of personal curiosity.

Kent's face crinkled. "I'm not telling you."

I texted Denise. [Any luck with the database search?]

[Got three potential matches. I'll text you their info.]

A few moments later, my phone buzzed with three mugshots of men who fit the description of Jesse. I showed them to Kent. "Are any of these the guy?"

Kent nodded. "This one," he said, pointing to the middle picture.

"Jesse Dunlop," I said.

"I say we go pay him a visit," JD said.

"Nobody can know that I talked to you," Kent said, his face bathed in panic. "He's got cartel connections. I don't want to end up at the bottom of the ocean."

"You sure you don't know where the submarine is?" I asked.

Kent shook his head.

I'm not so sure I believed him.

"We'll be in touch," I said. "Don't leave town."

We slid out of the booth and left the *Salty Dawg*. The bright sun squinted my eyes as we stepped into the parking lot and hopped into the Porsche. Jack drove to the Mar Vista Apartments. It was a nice upscale mid-rise with secure parking and a rooftop pool. It didn't have quite the amenities of the Nautilus or the Trident Tower.

Jesse Kennedy had priors for DUI, possession of a controlled substance, and a few other misdemeanors. I figured he was trying to step up from being a mid-level player to moving serious amounts of cocaine.

I buzzed a random number on the call box, identified myself as a sheriff's deputy, and somebody buzzed us in. We crossed the lobby to the elevator, and JD hit the call button. It lit up, and a moment later, the doors slid open. We stepped aboard and zipped up to the third floor.

I put a fist against #310.

Footsteps shuffled down the foyer, and a gruff voice filtered through the door. "Who is it?"

"Coconut County. We'd like to talk to you for a moment."

He didn't respond.

40

"You got a warrant?" Jesse shouted through the door.

"Why would we need a warrant?" I asked. "We just want to talk."

"About what?"

"Why don't you open the door, and we can have a face-to-face?"

"Why are you here?"

"Well, it seems you scared the bejesus out of Mrs. Cook."

"Who?"

"You know who. Garrison's wife."

"I don't know what you're talking about."

"You didn't go over to Pirates' Cove and threaten her?" I asked in a snide tone.

"Like I said, I don't know what you're talking about. This conversation is over."

"Oh, that hurts my feelings."

"Get used to it."

I snickered, and we headed back down the hallway toward the elevator. I called Isabella. "I think Jesse Dunlop's burner phone is about to pop up on the grid. We just rattled his cage. I would imagine he'll make a phone call to Garrison and ask why two cops showed up at his door."

"I'll keep an eye out."

I ended the call before I stepped aboard the elevator. We plummeted down to the lobby and made our way to the Porsche. We climbed inside and hung out for a moment, surveilling the building. If my hunch was right, Jesse wouldn't make a call from his apartment.

Sure enough, 10 minutes later, he pulled out of the parking garage in a matte black Dodge Charger with an aftermarket exhaust. The engine rumbled.

We pulled out of the visitors' lot and followed, keeping our distance. I don't think he was looking for a Porsche to be tailing him.

We followed him through the streets until he pulled into a parking garage at the mall.

We pulled into a lot across the street.

Jesse wasn't as dumb as he looked in his mug shot. Going to a public place and making a call on a burner phone would make it hard to link him to the phone. There were hundreds of other devices in the area, all pinging the cell tower. Even driving down the road, his car could be captured by a Department of Transportation camera. The timestamp on the image could be compared to the GPS data of the burner. It would take some doing to coordinate all the data, but it could be done.

When you're involved in illegal activity, you don't want your communications to be connected to you in any way. It's really easy to screw up and make a mistake. To give away your identity. Buy a burner phone with a credit card, and it can be tracked back to you. Turn it on at home, and it can be tracked back to you. Connect to a wireless network in your name, it could be linked to you. We carry with us mobile tracking devices and microphones capable of spying on our every word, and we pay for the privilege. It's been the biggest boon to the intelligence community ever.

The department didn't have the capabilities to track cell phones in real-time and intercept phone calls, but Isabella did. It wasn't exactly legal, and we couldn't use the evidence she gathered in a court of law, but it could provide valuable insight.

Isabella texted. *[Jesse's burner popped up on the grid.]*

She confirmed the location and monitored the call. A few minutes later, she sent me an MP3 of the conversation between Jesse and Garrison.

"You want to explain to me why two cops showed up at my door," Jesse growled.

"I don't know," Garrison stammered.

"You think I'm fucking around? I've been really cool about this. I presented an opportunity that can make you a lot of money. But you keep being difficult. You're trying the limits of my patience. I don't think you realize who you are dealing with."

"You shouldn't have threatened my wife."

"It's not me you've gotta worry about. There are people counting on us to deliver."

"Us?"

"Promises were made."

"I never agreed to anything," Garrison said through gritted teeth. "I said I'd think about it."

"I told them you were on board. Now, unfortunately, we're committed."

"You're insane."

"I'm a visionary."

"Have you ever heard the phrase *under promise, over-deliver*? It seems you've over-promised."

"Well, now we have to deliver. The cartel is expecting it. So you better get with the program. I'm not gonna make any more threats. I don't have to. Believe me, the cartel will find us and kill us both if we don't do as promised."

I didn't know if Jesse was just bullshitting Garrison or if he was telling the truth. Either way, it was effective.

"One time," Garrison said in a resigned tone. "We make one trip, pick up your cargo, then I'm out."

"See, was that so hard? We could have saved so much trouble. We leave tonight."

"What!?"

"You heard me."

"We need more time to prep."

"Bullshit. Fuel up and be ready to go by 2 AM."

"It's not that easy. Everyone is looking for the sub."

"Not my problem."

"Who are you working for?" Garrison asked.

"I'm not working for anybody. I'm working with certain individuals."

"I like to know who I'm getting into bed with."

"What I tell you is all you need to know."

There was a moment of silence.

"Where's the submarine now?" Jesse asked.

"Meet me at Pirates' Cove. We'll go to the sub together."

"Just a word of caution. Anything happens to me, the cartel will come looking for you," Jesse said. "I'll be there at 2 AM. Be ready."

The audio clip ended.

"I think we need to be waiting at the marina for them," JD said. "Follow them out to the sub."

"Then what? Arrest Garrison for possession of stolen property? Search the sub, which he's probably scrubbed by now."

A mischievous grin tugged Jack's lips. "I have a plan."

41

Wе prepped our tactical gear and loaded it into the new wake boat—night vision optics with infrared, a sniper rifle, a few AR-15s, and lots of extra magazines, just in case.

We cruised around the coastline and waited near Pirates' Cove. We had a few fishing poles to provide cover.

It was a little after 2 AM when Jesse arrived in a 25-foot center console with twin outboards. It had a navy hull with white trim. He cruised to the dock. Garrison waited for him with a black duffel bag slung over his shoulder, loaded with supplies and gear. He climbed into the boat as I watched through the optics.

They idled out of the marina, and when they passed the breakwater, Jesse throttled up, bringing the boat on plane. The twin outboards spit foam, and the small boat carved through the inky swells, howling into the night.

JD and I ditched the fishing poles, and he cranked up the engine. We kept our distance as we raced after them. I sat at the bow, the boat bouncing across the water. Mists of salt water sprayed, and the briny air swirled.

We followed them out to Crystal Key. The small island was once home to an ambitious resort project that never reached completion. The remnants of elevated cabanas dotted the island, and the small dock was in disarray. A few hurricanes had decimated the place, and the island worked at a feverish pace to reclaim the grounds. The once luxury stilted bungalows were like shanties.

Garrison had docked the sub and covered it with a tarp. The boat had been hiding in plain sight, yet no one had discovered it.

Jack killed the engine, and the boat slumped into the swells. We drifted on the onyx water, the stars glimmering above, the moon casting a pale glow, shimmering on the water.

I watched through the optics as Jesse navigated the boat to the dock and Garrison tied off. They climbed out, unloaded their gear, pulled the tarp away, then boarded the submarine, loading their gear aboard.

I figured if we tried to bring Garrison down now, the only thing that would stick would be possession of stolen property.

JD had contacted an old Navy buddy that worked with the Joint Interagency Task Force. The plan was to let them embark on their journey, albeit with a little surveillance.

The promise of a future bust with one of the largest payloads in recent history was enough to garner serious attention and resources.

If these guys came back with a thousand kilos of coke, we might be able to turn this into a win-win scenario. Not only would we have enough to put Garrison and Jesse away for a considerable portion of their natural lives, we might even ensnare a few cartel members in the process.

Garrison cast off the lines then climbed down the hatch and sealed the submarine. The black sub navigated away from the dock, and we followed the boat out to sea.

JD kept in touch with the task force. High above, a Poseidon P8 was ready to do its business.

Based on the Boeing 737, the P8 was the Navy's ultimate submarine hunter. It was capable of low-altitude cruising and had a vast array of radar and surveillance equipment. They could spot and track a submarine periscope from the air. Sensors could detect diesel exhaust. Radar could track ships up to 300 miles away. And if necessary, it could deploy a torpedo to take out a submarine.

The P8 deployed sonobuoys from above. The arrays splashed into the water and relayed acoustic signals back to the aircraft.

Every vessel at sea has its own sonic signature—the way the engines rumble, the sound the propellers make, the sound as it moves through the water. Each sonic fingerprint is recorded, cataloged, and can be used to identify the ship. Like a fingerprint, no two are the same. The vast array of acoustic devices throughout the ocean creates a wide net to capture sonic signals.

Running at the surface on diesel power, Julian's submarine made a lot of noise. Silent running under the surface, using electric power, would be more difficult to track, though not impossible. The boat would have to spend the majority of its time on the surface recharging the batteries.

We followed the homemade submarine until the conning tower slipped below the surface of the water and disappeared. It was a hell of an adventure these two idiots were setting off on. I gave it a 50-50 chance they would make it back alive. All kinds of things could go wrong. And even if they made it to Colombia, getting crossways with the cartel was always a possibility. The cartel might want to confiscate the submarine for themselves and cut out the middlemen.

They were taking a big risk all the way around.

With the sub's sonic signature now in the database, the task force would be able to recognize it when it re-entered local waters. And, when they surfaced, we'd be there to spoil the party—if things went according to plan.

We returned to Coconut Key, and JD navigated the wake boat into the slip. By that time, the sun was creeping over the horizon. I tied off, and we grabbed the gear and loaded it aboard the *Avventura*.

It was time for a little shut-eye.

I had just nodded off when Denise called. "Lab work came back on the baggie of coke you found in your guest stateroom."

42

"Sydney Voss," Denise said. "She handled that baggie at some point in time. Her prints were on file from a DUI. Residue in that bag was similar but not the same chemically as the others."

My brow furrowed. "We're talking two different batches of tainted drugs?"

"Maybe. Hard to say."

I thanked her for the info and went back to sleep. I was beat. We'd catch up with Sydney later.

It seemed like I had just shut my eyes again when Denise called around noon. "Hey, you two need to get down to the hospital."

"What's going on?"

"Gunshot victim was dropped off at the ER. Matches the description of Isaiah Turner. He was in sepsis upon arrival and is in surgery now. Didn't have any ID on him. Daniels wants you to check it out and confirm."

"We're on it."

I pulled myself out of bed, showered, and headed down to the galley after I got dressed. I grilled up breakfast, which was really lunch. I banged on the hatch to JD's stateroom while bacon sizzled in the pan. He grunted and groaned, finally staggering out about the time it was ready.

We chowed down, then took the Porsche up to the hospital.

The receptionist told us Isaiah was still in surgery.

We sat in the crowded waiting room with a bunch of sickly looking people. Long faces, bruises and abrasions, sniffling noses, broken bones, and hacking coughs.

I didn't like this place one bit, and neither did anybody else.

Dr. Parker emerged an hour later wearing teal scrubs and a surgical cap. A mask covered his face.

"What's the verdict?" I asked.

"The kid's gonna make it. He got lucky."

Dr. Parker told me he had removed the bullet from Isaiah's abdomen. It had lodged into the muscle around the iliac crest, but it hadn't punctured the descending colon. The suspect was on vancomycin—a pretty heavy-duty antibiotic.

"He's in a recovery unit now, then we'll move him to an intermediate care unit. He's not really able to answer questions right now. Might want to give it some time."

"I just need to positively ID him as our suspect."

Dr. Parker agreed and escorted us through the double doors and down a maze of hallways to the recovery unit. Monitors blipped with heartbeats and displayed vital statistics.

Nurses scurried about. Patients lay in beds separated by curtains. There were a lot of groggy faces.

I took one look at the perp. It was him, alright. Isaiah wouldn't be going anywhere, anytime soon, but I placed a cuff around his wrist and attached it to the bed rail.

"Is that absolutely necessary?" a nurse asked with an annoyed face.

"Ma'am, this kid has killed two people. He's been on the run for a while. I'm not taking a chance that he kills anyone else."

She gave me a disapproving look. "He'll have to go to the bathroom at some point in time."

I dug into my pocket and detached the key from my key ring, and gave it to her. "He's a dangerous individual. Don't let your guard down."

She took the key and slipped it into a pocket.

I don't think my words of caution sunk in with her. She'd seen the results of trauma, but I doubted she'd seen first-hand what one human being could do to another.

Lying in a hospital bed, barely conscious, Isaiah looked innocent and helpless. He didn't look like the kind of guy that could kill two people in cold blood. Sometimes, the unassuming ones are the most dangerous.

Though, in his current state, he wasn't much of a threat.

When we reviewed the surveillance footage from a camera at the entrance of the ER, it showed a black sedan pull to the curb. The door opened, and Isaiah was dumped out. The car sped away, the license plate obscured with duct tape.

Isaiah was looking at life in prison, and I guess his gang associates didn't want a corpse on their hands.

As we were leaving the ER, Paris Delaney and her crew arrived. She stood in front of the hospital with the emergency sign in the background as the camera lensed her up.

There was a leak in the department, and I'm sure she paid a pretty penny for the info. Guys in the department risked their lives every day for a pittance. Barely enough to make ends meet in this town. It wasn't surprising that someone was supplementing their income by feeding stories to the ambitious blonde.

"Wanted fugitive, Isaiah Turner, was brought to the hospital on the brink of death," Paris said. "I'm told he is in stable condition and is in custody. Here's Deputy Wild now." She turned her attention to me. "What can you tell us?"

The camera swung in my direction.

"I think you know as much as we do. I can tell you Isaiah Turner's reign of terror is over. He won't be hurting anyone anymore."

I stepped out of frame, feeling relieved that the situation was over.

Out of the corner of my eye, I caught sight of Jace Hill entering the ER. The door slid open, and he stepped inside. Isaiah had murdered his best friend, Curtis King. He was hell-bent on revenge. There could only be one reason he was here.

I alerted JD, and we ran toward the entrance.

43

"Jace!" I shouted as we rushed back into the ER.

He craned his neck, looking over his shoulder. His face tightened, and he took off running.

His sister had informed us he was on the prowl for Isaiah. We'd arrested him for possession of marijuana not long ago, primarily to get him off the street before he did something stupid. He had a gun at the time, which compounded the offense. Now, he was out on bail, and I figured he had a gun on him. He wouldn't want to get caught again.

Jace burst through the double doors and sprinted down the hallway, dodging nurses and patients. His sneakers slapped against the floor.

JD and I gave chase.

The kid darted away and smacked into a nurse rushing out of a patient's room.

She tumbled to the ground.

Jace kept racing down the hallway. He burst through another set of double doors.

I ran to the nurse and helped her to her feet. "Are you okay?"

She nodded, frazzled.

JD continued after the perp, and I fell in behind him.

We pushed through another set of double doors, dashing into the main lobby of the hospital. I glanced around and saw Jace outside, racing under the carport. The automated glass doors slid open as we followed him.

Jace ran down the main entry drive of the hospital.

My chest heaved, and my legs drove me forward. The wind tousled my hair.

Jace darted across the street.

The tires squealed, and horns honked.

A red convertible Porsche almost took out his kneecaps. Jace managed to avoid the collision, dancing around the front end of the vehicle.

"Watch where you're going, fucking asshole!" the driver shouted.

The red Porsche belonged to Logan Shea. My eyes rounded with surprise when I caught a glimpse of his passenger, Sydney Voss.

Jace crossed to the median, and the red Porsche sped away.

Jace continued across the other lanes, dodging traffic. But I was more preoccupied with the two in the Porsche.

We caught our breath on the sidewalk, cars whizzing by.

"Are you thinking what I'm thinking?" JD said.

I nodded and pulled my phone from my pocket. I called the sheriff. "I think we need to post a deputy at the hospital to watch Isaiah Turner."

"Are you volunteering?"

"I think Jace Hill came here with the intention of assassinating him. In the meantime, I think we're catching a break on the Tara DeVille case."

"I thought that was already settled."

"There may be more layers to this onion."

I ended the call, texted Isabella, and asked her to track Sydney's phone.

We hustled back to Jack's Porsche, climbed in, and JD pulled out of the parking lot.

Isabella called and said Sydney's phone was heading east on Cypress.

Jack sped in that direction, trying to catch up. A few twists and turns later, Isabella said, "They're pulling into the lot at the *Seven Seas*."

It took us a few minutes to get to the posh hotel. By the time we did, Logan had parked, and the couple had disappeared down a private path to the cabanas. He'd skipped the valet, trying to avoid attention.

We parked a few spaces away from his car.

Isabella had tracked them to the cabana named the Conch Castle, and we hustled to catch up with them.

The bungalows were popular among celebrity types looking to get away. Secluded, with private entrances, they were perfect for little trysts and drug-filled weekends.

We hovered at the entrance to the Conch Castle. I put my ear to the door, listening to the conversation inside. It was too muffled to decipher.

A mischievous glint sparkled in JD's eyes. "I'll be right back."

He slipped around the side of the bungalow. I figured he was heading toward the back patio to get a look inside. This unit backed up to the beach.

I banged on the door, and footsteps drew near. The peephole flickered. Through the door, Logan shouted, "What do you want?"

"I'd like a few words with Sydney," I said.

He hesitated for a long moment. "Who?"

"No need to play games. I know Sydney's in there."

"I don't know what you're talking about."

"I'd hate for the paparazzi and the local news to show up. I'm sure your wife would love to know about your affair with yet another adult film star. Pretty sure the studio would get a kick out of it too."

A moment later, the door opened. Logan scowled at me.

"See, that wasn't so hard," I said.

"This is harassment," Logan said. "My personal life is none of your concern."

"Well, it is when it involves a crime."

"What crime?"

Sydney lingered in the foyer behind him, her nervous eyes looking over his shoulder at me.

"Maybe you haven't been keeping up," I said. "Tara DeVille is dead. Dick Steele almost died of an overdose."

Logan interrupted. "I heard on the news Billy Diamond was implicated."

"New evidence has come to light."

"What new evidence?"

"Sydney's fingerprints are on a baggie of cocaine that was found in Tara DeVille's stateroom."

"What!?" Sydney exclaimed with a twisted face.

"Care to explain how your prints got there?"

She started to say something, then stopped.

"You know what I think?"

They looked at me with dumb faces, fear creeping into their eyes.

"I think you both had a problem and came to a mutual solution." I looked Logan dead in the eyes. "Tara was pregnant, and you needed her to go away." Then my laser eyes aimed at Sydney. "And you took care of your main rival."

Sydney scoffed. "You think I gave her coke laced with fentanyl? That's ridiculous. And you can't prove it, anyway."

In my experience, guilty people challenge you to prove a fact. The innocent are much more likely to be transparent.

"Billy Diamond tried to kill Dick," Sydney said. "Tara got into Dick's stash. End of story."

"Maybe so. But how did your prints get on the baggie?"

44

"We're done talking now," Logan said before he slammed the door and twisted the deadbolt.

The two got into a heated discussion. Low voices growled at each other as they moved away from the door.

I pulled my phone from my pocket and texted Paris Delaney. This time, I decided to be the leaker. [You'll find Logan Shea and Sydney Voss in the Conch Castle at the Seven Seas. Might make for a good story. You're welcome.]

She texted back a moment later. *[Thanks for the heads up. He gets around, doesn't he?]*

[Seems that way.]

I told her about Sydney Voss's prints on the baggie.

[So, she's a person of interest?]

[Yes. You didn't hear this from me.]

[Hear what?]

I knew I could trust Paris to protect her sources.

I walked a few paces away from the door and waited for JD.

He emerged from the alley between the cabana a moment later with a grin on his face. He joined me and said, "Dip-shits had the sliding glass door open on the patio." He lifted his phone and jiggled it excitedly. "Take a look at this."

We moved farther away from the cabana, and he replayed the video he'd captured, hiding in the shrubs by the patio. We couldn't use this as evidence. They had a reasonable expectation of privacy in the hotel room, and we didn't have a warrant.

"Would you just relax?" Sydney hissed.

"How could you do something so stupid?"

"Stupid?" she asked, her tone sharpening.

"They have your fingerprints!"

"Big fucking deal."

"It is a big fucking deal. They're going to be on us like stink on shit. This is the last thing I need."

"I don't know what you're worried about. They can't tie anything to you."

"Not unless you start talking."

"I'm not talking."

Logan glared at her.

"What am I gonna say? Logan gave me the coke to kill Tara? It would be my word against yours. And I wouldn't do that to you, anyway." Her tone softened, and she moved close, wrapping her arms around his neck. "We stick together, and there's nothing they can do to us."

She planted a juicy kiss on him, and the two melted into each other. It wasn't long before she was on her knees, Logan's shorts around his ankles.

JD said, "I don't know about you, but those don't strike me as two innocent individuals."

It wasn't long before Paris Delaney and her news crew arrived, waiting to ambush the couple as they stepped out of the cabana. She flashed an appreciative grin as we crossed paths. "Listen, I need to talk to you about something when we have more time."

"Is this about that favor?"

"It's important."

She continued toward the bungalow, and we headed to the parking lot. We climbed into the Porsche, drove to *Diver Down*, and took a seat at the bar to watch the festivities.

Teagan noticed our mischievous grins. "What are you two up to?"

"You'll see," I said.

Her suspicious eyes flicked between the two of us as she poured two glasses of whiskey.

We perused the menus and shot the shit with the teal-eyed beauty. Jack ordered the conch chowder to start and yellowtail snapper with a lemon and parsley sauce. I ordered the seared scallops in a key lime ginger sauce.

Paris Delaney's breaking report appeared on the flatscreen behind the bar. The cameraman filmed Logan as he tried to sneak out of the cabana. The crew had hidden around the corner and ambushed him as he headed down the path to his car.

"How do you respond to allegations of your involvement in the death of Tara Deville?"

Logan's face went stiff, and the color drained. Then his cheeks flushed with rage. He continued walking, trying to evade the tenacious blonde.

"Can you tell me about your relationship with Sydney Voss?"

Logan scurried away, and the camera lens focused back on the cabana. Sydney was still inside, presumably.

Paris stepped in front of the lens. "An anonymous source shared with us this disturbing video of what appears to be Logan Shea and Sydney Voss discussing their involvement in the suspicious overdose of adult film star Tara DeVille.

I can't say how Paris got the clip that JD recorded on his cell phone, but it appeared on the flatscreen. It made the two look guilty, to say the least.

The segment cut back to Paris at the *Seven Seas*. "No arrests have been made, but the sheriff's department is investigating the case. We'll keep you updated as this story develops. I'm Paris Delaney, and you heard it from me first."

The anchor in the news studio attempted to sound sincere when she said, "Shocking allegations. In other news..."

JD grinned and lifted his glass.

We clinked and sipped the fine whiskey.

It wasn't long after the segment had aired that I got a call from Summer, the makeup artist from *Yacht Bunnies 2*.

45

"There was a lot going on that day," Summer said. "After watching that news report with Paris Delaney, it jogged my memory. I think I saw Sydney enter Tara's stateroom."

"You *think*, or you *know*?"

"Yeah, I saw her go into the stateroom. At first, I thought there was going to be a catfight. But then Sydney said something about a peace offering."

This would have been good information to have earlier, but better late than never. "I need you to come down to the station and make a sworn affidavit."

She agreed, and we met her half an hour later.

I filled out an application for a warrant, and by the next morning, we had one. I didn't think Sydney was going to give us much trouble, but we took Erickson and Faulkner to her apartment.

She lived in the *Estuary*. It was a nice place, on par with the *Delphine*. I put a fist against the door and shouted, "Coconut County! We have a warrant."

The property manager had given me a key, but the deadbolt was latched. Erickson and Faulkner were about to break down the door when the latch twisted and Sydney opened up.

I displayed the warrant and told her to "Turnaround. Put your hands behind your back."

"I didn't do anything," she protested.

"Do it. Now!"

She complied, and I smacked the cuffs around her wrists, then escorted her to the sofa. I told her to take a seat while JD and the deputies searched the apartment. They looked in drawers, the nightstand, bathroom, the closet.

She didn't have any drugs on hand. She must have flushed them. There was a pack of rolling papers and a tray with some scraps of weed on the nightstand by the bed, but not much else. No cocaine. No fentanyl.

"You have the right to remain silent..." I said as I escorted her out of the apartment.

We took the elevator down to the lobby, and I stuffed her into the back of a squad car. She was taken to the station, processed, and printed.

We filled out after-action reports, then attempted to have a conversation in the interrogation room.

Sydney was in tears when we entered. JD and I took a seat across the table from her. Mascara stained her cheeks, and tears streamed down.

"We've got your prints on the baggie, and we've got a witness that saw you interacting with Tara before her death."

"A lot of people interacted with Tara that day."

"There's a video of you circulating where you practically admit to the murder. Whether that evidence will be admissible in court, I don't know. But I can tell you that every potential juror has probably seen it."

"So, you're saying I won't get a fair trial."

"I'm saying you're going to be spending a long time in a 6x8 cell."

She didn't like the idea. Not many people did.

"Logan's gonna walk away from this whole thing," I said. "We've got a good circumstantial case against you. Logan... Not so much."

I let that sink in for a moment.

"You cooperate, testify against your co-conspirator, and I'm sure we can get a reduced sentence."

She was silent for a long moment.

"You can't prove anything. I don't know how you got that video, but unless you had a warrant, it's inadmissible. If this thing goes to trial, my attorney will petition for a change of venue now that the entire jury pool has been tainted."

Sydney Voss was no dummy.

She lifted her nose high and smiled. "And when this whole thing is over, I'm gonna walk away with a book deal, a movie deal, and maybe even a talk show."

JD and I exchanged an annoyed glance. With the way society was, she was probably right. It seemed the quickest way to fame was to become a criminal.

"I'm not answering any more questions without an attorney," she said.

I gave an ominous shrug and pushed away from the table.

I knocked on the door, and a guard buzzed us out. Sheriff Daniels joined us in the hallway, having watched from the observation room.

"Please tell me you got something more on her and that scumbag movie star?"

"We'll keep on it," I said.

Daniels frowned and shook his head. "What about the Evangeline Everhart case?"

"Nothing. My guess is she's at the bottom of the ocean."

"You can't find the missing girl. You let two clowns take off in a submarine headed to Colombia, one of which is probably a murderer, and you don't have a solid case against the porn star."

"Is this your idea of a pep talk?" JD asked.

"I should have pulled you two off this case. It's not going to look good if this one goes unsolved."

"Give it time," I said.

He gave me a look, then marched away.

I shared a glance with JD.

Paris Delaney buzzed my phone. "Hey, what's going on?"

"You know, the usual."

"Just wanted to say thanks again for that tip. That story is one of our most watched, and that video already has more than a million views. All the traffic damn near crashed the server."

"Congratulations."

"Did you hear?"

"Hear what?"

"The studio issued a statement, distancing themselves from Logan. His contract has been canceled, and his wife kicked him out of the house. Ironically, he's staying back at the *Seven Seas*. I have it on good authority he's in the Paradise Cabana. Care to give me a heads up when you're going to arrest him?"

"I don't have enough to arrest him. That video is not admissible. I need direct evidence of them conspiring to kill Tara DeVille."

"I'll see if he's willing to come on camera and do an interview."

"I doubt it."

"He needs to set the record straight. I'll give him an opportunity to clear his name. Maybe he says something incriminating on camera."

"I'm sure he's lawyered up by now, and no lawyer worth their salt would let him do that."

"Never underestimate people's ego. Logan Shea is a narcissist. His whole world has collapsed. He's desperate right about now. I'll give him enough rope to hang himself."

"Bring me some usable evidence, and you might get back on my good side."

"Was I ever on your good side?"

"I assert my Fifth Amendment privilege."

She laughed.

The next morning, Sydney was indicted for capital murder, and bail was set at a million dollars. Nobody rushed to spring her out of jail, so she'd sit in the county pod until trial. She had burned through whatever money she earned as an adult film star as fast as it came in.

Logan struck me as a high-strung guy in general. This kind of pressure had to push him to the brink. From what I knew of his personality, I figured he would turn to drugs and alcohol. If we stayed on him long enough, and kept dialing up the pressure, he might crack and do something stupid.

I had a plan.

46

W e recruited Kirk, a corrections officer in the pod. He was more than eager to participate.

We had Paris run a story. She went on air and said, "Sources close to the Tara DeVille investigation say that a co-conspirator is close to negotiating a deal to testify against other suspects."

It was completely bogus. *Unnamed* media sources are never reliable.

We wanted to put Logan on edge. He'd been staying at the *Seven Seas* since the debacle went down. Logan had been taking it easy and staying within the hotel compound. He'd been seen at the pool and on the beach, wearing sunglasses and a hat, trying to stay incognito. In the evenings, he could be found in the bar. He wasn't opposed to picking up a working girl or two. A different kind of room service.

We put a wireless spy cam on Kirk. From an app on my phone, we could monitor and record the interaction.

Kirk approached Logan in the bar one night and took a seat next to him at the counter. Logan was talking to a young blonde who was a regular in the bar. We'd seen her there working numerous times before. I didn't know how much money Logan had in the bank, but at the rate he was going through hookers and blow, he'd be indigent by the end of the year.

"I can help you with your problem," Kirk muttered to Logan.

Logan ignored him, preoccupied with the blonde.

Kirk tapped him on the shoulder. "You might want to listen to me."

Logan's face crinkled. "Who the fuck are you?"

"Your salvation."

"Excuse me?"

"You have a problem. I can solve that problem."

"The only problem I've got is you interrupting my evening." Logan returned his attention to the blonde.

"You ready to get out of here?" the sultry blonde asked.

"Absolutely," Logan said.

"Sydney's about to turn state's evidence," Kirk muttered. He slid off the bar stool and patted Logan on the shoulder as he walked away. "Good luck with that."

Logan's irritation soon gave way to concern. "Hey, wait a minute!"

Kirk was a big, imposing figure. 6'2", 240 pounds, with the body of a lineman. He lumbered toward the exit, then stopped, his back to Logan.

"Have a seat," Logan said. "I'll buy you a drink."

Kirk hesitated a moment, then turned around and resumed his position at the bar next to Logan. He ordered another round of drinks. The bartender grabbed a bottle of top-shelf whiskey and filled two glasses. He slid them across the counter.

Logan picked up his glass and offered a quick toast to Kirk. The troubled star asked, "Where are you getting your information?"

"I have sources."

Logan gave him a look.

"I'm a corrections officer inside the jail."

Logan squirmed, a little uneasy.

"Obviously, I could get in a lot of trouble talking to you about this," Kirk said.

"What are we talking about?"

"An answer to your prayers."

Logan turned to his blonde companion. "Sugar, can you give us a minute?"

She lifted a sassy eyebrow at him. "I guess." She slinked away and found some other lonely man to entice.

Logan surveyed Kirk with caution. "Let's hear about this *solution*."

"Without a certain witness, the state doesn't have a case against you. Am I right?"

"I don't think the state has a case against me, anyway. I'm innocent."

"Of course you are. But innocent people go to jail all the time. Wouldn't you like an insurance policy?"

Logan stared at Kirk for a moment, then glanced around to see if anyone was listening to their conversation.

"We're talking *life* insurance?"

"You could call it that," Kirk said.

"Is there a *death* benefit?"

"Considerable."

"What's the premium?"

Kirk grabbed a napkin, pulled a pen from his breast pocket, and scribbled a number. He slid it across the counter to Logan.

His eyes rounded as he read it, and he whistled. "That's a lot of money."

"Can you put a price on freedom?"

Logan considered it. The answer was obvious.

"I'd ask if you were some kind of cop," Logan said. "But you're some kind of cop. How do I know this isn't a setup?"

"You want to check me for a wire?"

"Yeah, I do."

Kirk unbuttoned his shirt and revealed his hairy barrel chest. "See anything you like?"

Logan frowned at him.

Kirk buttoned his shirt. The camera was hidden in a pen that was clipped to his breast pocket.

Logan never paid any attention to it.

"So, how would this work?" Logan asked.

"You'd make a cash payment, half up front, and I'd take care of the rest."

"And this *insurance policy* would pay out before this thing goes to trial?"

"You'd see the benefit within a week."

"If you think I'm going to trust some random stranger that approaches me in a bar..."

"What choice do you really have?"

Logan frowned. "I need some time to think about it. Properly vet the situation."

"Take as much time as you need. It's your life. Word in the pod is she's about to spill the beans."

"What kind of deal are they giving her?"

"Involuntary manslaughter. 15 years."

Logan cringed. "That's a long time."

"It's better than life."

"Have you done this kind of thing before?"

Kirk chuckled. "How about you get on the web, do a search for inmate deaths? Tell me how many hits you get."

"I'm supposed to believe you're responsible for all of those?"

"I'm not responsible. I never lift a finger. But it's amazing what an inmate will do for a little commissary. If you're lucky, you'll never find out what it's like inside. But god forbid you go away. They're gonna love a guy like you."

Logan's face stiffened, and he swallowed hard.

"Call that number if you decide you want to move forward. By the way, I hear they're moving her to protective custody soon. Makes things more complicated."

Kirk gulped the last swig of his drink and left the bar, patting Logan on the shoulder one more time as he passed.

Logan's eyes followed him with suspicion.

I wasn't sure he would take the bait.

47

I t didn't take much convincing to get Logan's wife to authorize access to his phone records. In his abrupt departure from the residence, he'd left his tablet behind, and she gave us access. Despite numerous calls and texts, there was nothing incriminating between Logan and Sydney. No suspicious emails. No talk of murdering Tara.

We needed solid, admissible evidence of a conspiracy. Without it, Logan would likely walk.

A couple weeks went by with no activity.

Then we got a call from the Joint Task Force. They picked up the sub on radar while it was surface cruising. The Coast Guard tried to interdict them, but they submerged. The task force kept tabs on the sub all the way in. It was an easy target for the P8.

It was an expensive operation for the Task Force. But the potential for a high-value bust seemed like a good allocation of resources. And everyone wanted to justify their operating budget. In the scheme of things, it was a drop in the bucket.

Official stats had the Task Force interdicting 10% of the total drugs flowing into the country.

The reality was much different.

Law enforcement was only catching a fraction of the imports. There was no way to track and stop everything. As far as the cartels were concerned, the losses were just a cost of doing business. An unregulated tax.

The truth is, nobody wanted the drug trade to stop. It was too lucrative on both sides. Entire agencies would crumble. Defense contractors would lose valuable deals. Somebody had to supply the airplanes, the boats, the weapons, the radar systems, and tracking devices. Not to mention the overall hit to the economy. Drug dealers bought flashy cars, boats, houses, and condominiums. They laundered money through banks and funneled money into political campaigns. Not to mention all the people on the take that looked the other way.

How do you really fight something like that?

It could seem futile at times. But we did what we could do. One day at a time, one bad guy at a time.

I sat at the bow of the wake boat, scanning the horizon with night vision opticals. The conning tower poked through the swells, and the submarine surfaced just north of Barracuda Key around midnight.

A few clouds drifted in the sky, and the full moon shimmered the inky water.

The P8 flew high overhead, and Coast Guard patrol boats waited in the wings. We were about half a mile away from the sub, drifting with the swells. The boat pitched and rolled, and the waves lapped against the hull.

It wasn't long before a *Go Fast* boat approached the sub, skimming across the water, the massive outboards spitting a frothy wake. The boat pulled alongside the submarine and tied off.

That's when the real work began—unloading a ton of cocaine wrapped in black plastic bales and lugging them up the hatch. One by one, they were transferred onto the *Go Fast* boat.

The Task Force closed in.

JD took the helm and cranked up the engines. We plowed through the inky swells toward the midnight rendezvous. Defender class patrol boats advanced, and the MH60 Jayhawk pattered in the air above.

Adrenaline coursed through my veins, and my heart pumped. The thrill of the chase.

It didn't take the perps long to figure out they were under siege.

The guys in the *Go Fast* boat cut their losses. They cast off the lines, jumped into the boat, and cranked up the engine. The racing boat howled, spitting a rooster tail as it launched away from the submarine. It skimmed across the water and veered to avoid the approaching patrol boats.

It was too fast for us to keep up with.

One of the thugs in the boat started dumping the bales overboard, but that wasn't going to help their situation.

They were armed to the teeth with fully automatic weapons. Once the bales of cocaine were dumped overboard, a goon at the stern opened fire at the chasing patrol boats. Muzzle flash flickered, and bullets snapped through the air.

We closed in on the submarine while the Coast Guard pursued the *Go Fast* boat.

Garrison closed the hatch and sealed it just as we arrived. The vessel moved forward and prepared to submerge.

The Jayhawk fired a couple of warning shots across the bow of the *Go Fast* boat.

It did little to slow them down.

With the next round of shots, the .50 Cal took out the outboards.

The clatter of heavy weapons fire echoed through the night.

Bullets streaked through the air, peppering the engine cowlings with molten copper.

Bits of debris scattered, and the engines caught fire as fuel leaked onto hot manifolds.

Flames engulfed the engines, and black smoke billowed into the air, glowing the black water.

That was the end of the chase for the *Go Fast* boat.

The thugs quickly realized they were outgunned. They dropped their weapons and put their hands in the air as Coast Guard patrol boats surrounded them.

We cruised alongside the submarine as it moved forward on the surface. It wasn't the fastest thing in the world, but it could move in a direction that we couldn't.

Down.

The conning tower slowly descended into the swells and vanished with a swirl. Running on electric power, it would be a little harder to detect than when the diesels were clattering away. But with the P8 overhead, there was nowhere they could hide.

JD and I launched our sonar drone, and with a few taps of his cell phone, the device locked onto the submarine and followed it. That allowed us to navigate on the surface.

The drone followed the sub, and we followed the drone.

The sub headed back out to sea. I don't think Garrison had a plan. The electric power wouldn't last long. I was certain, after a journey like they'd been on, there wasn't enough fuel for an extended run. He probably thought he could get to international waters, but then what? No food, no water, no fuel. I couldn't see that working out too well.

48

A few miles into the chase, the conning tower pierced the surface. The sub had made an emergency ascent and lurched into the swells. A moment later, the hatch opened, and Garrison climbed out, coughing and hacking.

Jesse followed.

Black smoke funneled from the hatch.

We closed in, along with another patrol boat.

I shouldered an AR-15 and took aim at the thugs. "On the deck! Now! Face down!"

The waves crashed against the submarine. Jesse had a pistol in his hand and thought momentarily about resisting, then thought better of it. He tossed the weapon away and ate the deck.

JD pulled alongside the sub, and I leaped over the gunwale.

Two other petty officers joined me, and we cuffed the perps and transferred them to the patrol boat.

The acrid smoke filled the air, and I tried to avoid inhaling the fumes that were a mix of fuel, electronics, and whatever drugs they had left aboard. It was pretty noxious stuff.

Every shred of evidence aboard that sub was incinerated, but we had the bales of cocaine that were thrown overboard from the *Go Fast* boat. There was no doubt in my mind that all these clowns would spend at least 30 years in the can on federal drug trafficking charges.

The sub ended up on the bottom of the ocean, and the perps were taken back to the Sheriff's Department.

Paris Delaney and crew were on the dock, waiting for us to return. She filmed our arrival.

JD pulled the wake boat into a slip, and I tied off. I climbed to the dock and hustled to the news crew.

I pulled Paris aside. "Are you live?"

"No."

"I need a favor."

"Oh, you need a favor?"

"You can't break this story now."

"Why not?"

"Because I need to flip these guys and get to their boss. Otherwise, we're just taking out pawns."

"This is a great story, and I can break it first."

"What do you need from me?"

She took a deep breath and stared into my eyes.

"Who hooked you up with the Logan Shea story?" I said, holding it over her.

"We both benefited from that. Don't make it sound like you were doing that out of the goodness of your heart."

"Paris..."

She huffed. "Okay. Fine. I'll give you until the morning show. 7 AM."

That was only a few hours away.

"Give me a heads up before it runs. And don't show the perp's faces."

"Deal." Then she added, "Now you do one for me."

"What is it?"

"Promise you'll say *yes*. You and JD."

My brow crinkled. "I can't promise until I know what you're asking."

She took a deep breath, and her eyes misted. "It's about my niece. She's sick."

A heavy weight tugged at my chest.

"She's been diagnosed with a rare blood disease. Aplastic Anemia. The odds are literally one in a million. Her red blood cell count, white blood cell count, and platelets are low."

I frowned. "I'm sorry."

"She needs a bone marrow transplant, but we haven't found a good match. If she doesn't find a donor, she..." Her eyes teared up. "I'm asking everybody I know—"

"Of course. What do we have to do?"

"It's just a cheek swab. Register in the database. Then wait and see."

"That's not a favor, Paris. That's a given. Of course, we'll do whatever we can."

She smiled and gave me a hug, squeezing tight. She whispered, "Thank you."

She broke free and composed herself. "I'm going to run a story and make a call out to the general public for donors. With any luck..." she crossed her fingers.

"Just let me know how we do this."

She gave an appreciative nod. "I'll be in touch."

We shared a rare moment on the dock. It wasn't often that Paris's soft side came out. It lasted an instant, then she was back in ambition mode.

The Task Force guys were eager to pose for photos and footage with the bales of cocaine. They wanted their 15 minutes. It would make for good publicity.

The perps were processed and printed, and we filled out after-action reports. Once the traffickers had enough time to sweat it out in the interrogation rooms, JD and I tried to pry information out of them.

The thugs in the *Go Fast* boat wouldn't talk. They knew talking was likely a death sentence.

I wanted to know where the cocaine was going.

Our next chat was with Garrison. By the time we got to him, sweat beaded his forehead, and he fidgeted nervously in the tiny room.

"You have a lot of explaining to do," I said as I took a seat across the table from him.

"I was forced to help that maniac. I had no choice. He threatened my family. You know that!"

"You're going to tell me who your connection is. I want to know where the drugs were going."

"How should I know? Ask Jesse."

"I intend to." I paused. "Care to tell me how you came into possession of the submarine?"

He hesitated. "Jesse killed Julian. He forced me to pilot the sub."

"Bullshit," JD grumbled. "We know otherwise."

His eyes narrowed at JD.

"We know about the HMS Silverstone," I said.

Garrison's face crinkled. He stammered, "How do you know about that?"

"We know you killed Julian."

"What!? Where are you getting this crap from?"

"How many people knew about your discovery of the Silverstone?" I said.

Garrison's jaw tightened. "So you've been talking to Kent."

"He's willing to testify." I didn't know if he would or not, but I threw it out there, anyway.

"What good is his testimony? He's making the whole thing up. You can't prove anything."

"If you didn't kill Julian, how did you get the sub?"

His face tightened, and his nervous eyes flicked between the two of us. "I want to speak with my attorney."

I tried to hide my displeasure, but that was the end of the interview.

I pushed away from the table and moved to the door. We might not get him on the murder charge, but there was no way this guy was doing anything less than 30 years. So I didn't get too upset about it.

A guard buzzed us out, and we stepped into the hallway.

Daniels found us. "Deputies searched Garrison's boat. No sign of a 9mm handgun."

"I'm sure he disposed of it, or perhaps it was aboard the sub."

"Well, you two numbskulls like crazy adventures. Maybe you can dive down to the sub and see what you can recover."

I exchanged a look with JD. It sounded like fun.

We visited with Jesse before calling it a night. He didn't look nervous or scared. Just disappointed.

I took a seat across from him and smiled. "You've been arrested before. You know how this works."

He didn't say anything.

"Today's your lucky day."

His face wrinkled. "How's that?"

"You're in a position right now to save your ass. Despite all your shenanigans, you're a low man on the totem pole. A bit player in a B movie. A nobody. I don't really care about you."

"I don't care about you either," Jesse said.

"Your partner in the next room is the prime suspect in the murder of Julian Pierce. He's saying that you killed Julian."

Jesse scoffed. "I had nothing to do with that."

"I know you didn't kill Julian because a toll camera puts you in Pineapple Bay the night of Julian's murder."

Jesse smiled.

"You have a rare and fleeting opportunity. Do yourself a tremendous favor and cooperate."

"What's in it for me?"

"I'll talk to the US Attorney. Maybe you can walk away from all this."

"Clean?" he asked in disbelief.

"Maybe a little time."

"Define *little*?"

"This is a federal drug trafficking crime. Stiff penalties. You're dealing with the big boys."

We stared at each other for a moment.

"I want to know two things," I said. "Where the dope was going, and if Garrison said anything to you about the death of Julian Pierce."

He thought about it for a moment.

"I want a deal in writing."

"I'll see what I can do. But you gotta give me a little something as an appetizer."

He paused. "We spent a long time in a cramped space together. I think I know that guy pretty well by now."

"Tell me about your trip. Did he try to disrupt the voyage at any time? After all, you did kidnap him." I muttered aside, "By the way, that's another charge you're looking at on top of the others."

"Garrison was pretty resigned to his fate," Jesse said. "A single person can't handle that ship on a transoceanic voyage. We both wanted to stay alive. We needed each other, and we both knew it."

"Did he tell you why he killed Julian?"

"The topic of discussion came up."

"And...?"

"Well, I know the three of them were keeping some kind of secret. He didn't go into detail about that. But he did let it slip out that he was capable of murder. I think he was trying to intimidate me. I take the basic standpoint that everybody is capable of murder. You gotta watch your back."

"Did he say why he killed Julian?"

"Julian was having an affair with Garrison's wife. He's the father of their child. Not Garrison." Jesse laughed, amused by it all.

I exchanged a glance with JD.

Jesse wasn't the most credible witness in the world, but combined with Kent's testimony, I figured we had a pretty solid case.

"Did Garrison have a gun?"

"He had one stashed, but I took it away from him."

"Where is it now?"

"Bottom of the ocean."

"In the sub?"

Jesse nodded.

"What kind?"

"A 9mm."

I looked at JD again.

"Now tell me where the drugs were going," I said.

49

"Hugo Ortega," Jesse said.

"You dealt with him personally?" I asked.

"No. Nobody deals with Hugo. My contact is Miguel."

"What about the two guys in the Go Fast boat, Thomas and Raphael?"

"Errand boys."

"How do you know Miguel?"

"I met him in a club. I knew he worked for Hugo, so I offered my services. I told him I could get his product shipped at a better price."

"That's pretty bold, even though you didn't have the submarine secured."

"I'm a big believer in setting a deadline and forcing yourself to rise to the challenge."

"You rose to the challenge, alright. How did that work out for you?"

He scowled at me. "I'm gonna hand you the entire cartel. It's gonna work out for me just fine." Jesse smiled.

We had contacted the US attorney and brokered a deal. If Jesse gave us information that could take the cartel down, he'd walk away without so much as a slap on the wrist. And he'd probably get a TV deal out of it, if the cartel didn't kill him first.

"It doesn't sound like you can give us any more than Raphael or Thomas, and we already have them."

Jesse's smug grin faded. "I can get to Miguel. And Miguel can get to Hugo. Therefore, I can give you Hugo. Don't forget, I'm handing you a murderer as well."

"Do you have anything that can tie Hugo to this? Text messages, phone calls, emails?"

"I told you. I never spoke to him directly. But with everything that's happened recently, Miguel took a high-level position in the organization. He's Hugo's #1 right now."

My face tightened.

"At least you got a name," Jesse said. "Now you know who to focus on."

"We've had Hugo's name for a long time. We've never been able to get anything solid on him."

"Hey, man. That's not my problem. I'm doing my part."

"Right now, Hugo doesn't know you're in custody. You're gonna reach out to Miguel. Let him know you escaped with the sub and have some of the drugs. Tell him what happened and that you want to make good, but you need to talk to Hugo face-to-face because you're worried about retribution because of the missing product."

Jesse swallowed hard. "You want me to set Hugo up?"

"If you want to breathe free air, that's exactly what you'll do."

He looked uncomfortable. He fidgeted in his chair, his cockiness fading.

I gave him his cell phone and told him to make the call.

"Now?" he asked, growing nervous.

"Yes, now. Time is of the essence."

His shaky fingers dialed the number, and he put it on speaker. It rang a few times, and a gruff voice answered. It was not a voice that was pleased. The tone was low, calm, and direct. "What happened?"

"Cops were at the rendezvous. Someone tipped them off."

"Who?"

"I don't know."

"Where are Thomas and Raphael?"

Jesse looked at me for guidance.

I coached him.

"I don't know. Probably in custody. We took off and submerged. Got the hell out of Dodge. There were cops everywhere. Helicopters, patrol boats, you name it."

"And the cargo?"

"There's a slight problem. We were in the middle of unloading, so some of the cargo was lost."

"Some?"

"We have a little left."

There was a long silence on the other end of the line. "That's disappointing."

"You're telling me. Look, I want to get this to you as soon as possible and explain the situation to Hugo personally."

"Bring it to me."

"I gotta talk to Hugo. I need to make sure we're square on this. I don't need to be looking over my shoulder. This wasn't my fault."

"Where are you now?"

Jesse's throat tightened. "I called a buddy, and we transferred what was left to a boat, then scuttled the sub."

"Why would you scuttle the sub?"

"Slight mechanical problem."

There was another long pause.

"I'll call you back with a location shortly."

"I get a face-to-face with Hugo, right?"

"Be where I tell you when I tell you. Make sure you're not followed. Stay close to a phone."

Miguel ended the call.

Jesse looked panicked. "How's this gonna work out? I gotta have something to give them."

"Don't worry about that," I said.

He looked worried.

I texted Paris and asked her to keep Jesse's name out of her story.

Miguel called back 15 minutes later.

"Take the boat to Salt Point Harbor," Miguel said. "Tie it off in the empty slip next to the Wayfarer. Leave the keys in the boat, then walk away."

"That's it?" Jesse said.

"That's it."

"What about Hugo?"

"You will be contacted at a later time."

"I don't want to end up with a bullet in the back of my head."

"I said you'd be contacted."

"Alright. I'll be there as soon as I can."

Jesse ended the call. "Now what?"

We found a 28-foot center console that had been confiscated by the department during another drug seizure. It had twin outboards, a hardtop, and a teal hull with white trim.

We loaded several bales of cocaine aboard, stuffing the fore-deck and cockpit. We covered them with a tarp and placed a few wireless spy cams around the boat and one on Jesse. They were linked to a 5G transmitter, and I could access the cameras from an app on my phone. They were good for about 24 hours of run time.

Before we sent Jesse on his way, I told him, "If you do anything to tip them off, the deal is off the table."

He raised his hands innocently. "I'm going to drop the boat off like I'm supposed to."

"You try to run, and we'll find you."

"I'm not gonna run. But you better do something to keep me safe. When they find out I've ratted them out, it's not going to be pretty."

"Just play your part. You'll be taken care of."

I looked into his eyes for acknowledgment.

He nodded.

"After you drop off the boat, walk to the parking lot, pretend to call a ride share, and an undercover deputy will pick you up."

"Then what?"

"You'll be taken back to your apartment. You'll go about your life like everything is normal. If they think you've been compromised, this whole operation will be a bust."

I had Isabella text a spyware link to Jesse's phone. I down-loaded and installed an app on his phone that would give us remote access to the device. This time, it was all legal. We could turn the phone's mic into a listening device. I told Jesse to keep the phone with him at all times.

I gave him the keys to the boat, and he climbed aboard. We cast off the lines, and he idled out of the marina. We hopped into the wake boat and followed, keeping our distance.

Tango One was in the air and on standby. Daniels sent a couple undercover units over to *Salt Point* in unmarked cars.

We followed Jesse as he cruised over to drop off the goods. He idled through the marina, found the slip next to the *Wayfarer*, and tied off the boat. He climbed out and walked down the dock, casually glancing around.

I had no doubt that someone was watching. Maybe from another boat. Maybe from the parking lot. Hell, maybe a small drone hovered overhead. Hugo's people would be looking for a trap, if they were smart.

JD and I dropped anchor, rolling with the swells outside the marina. I kept an eye on things with night vision optics.

JD cast a line into the water, pretending to fish.

Jesse did as he was instructed. When he reached the parking lot, an unmarked car picked him up, and he climbed into the backseat. The deputy zipped away, and we continued to keep eyes on the marina.

There was no activity.

We were out there until the sun came up, and still nothing.

We figured we ought to move before someone got suspicious. The morning sun sparkled the water. Soon, Paris would air the details of her story.

We returned to the *Avventura* and tuned into Paris's breaking news segment on the morning show. Sure enough, Paris kept to her word and left out any details about Jesse.

The center console sat untouched in the marina for two days.

The batteries in the spycams died, but Daniels kept undercover surveillance on it round the clock. I don't know if somebody spotted the deputies, but it was taking a long time for Hugo's crew to make a move on the coke. Despite it being a fraction of the total shipment, it was still a huge amount of cocaine. If anyone stole the boat in the meantime, they'd be in for a hell of a surprise.

51

"Well, this situation just went from bad to worse," Daniels said when he called that evening.

"What happened?" I asked.

"You two need to get over to the Mar Vista Apartments. Jesse just got a special delivery."

I groaned.

"This whole case just slipped away," Daniels aid.

"We're on our way."

I caught JD up to speed, and we hustled across the island to the Mar Vista. Camera flashes spilled down the third-floor hallway as we hustled toward apartment #310. Dietrich hovered by the door, snapping photos. Deputies Mendoza and Robinson milled about in the hallway. Brenda hadn't arrived yet. A few curious neighbors gawked from their doorways.

Jesse lay in the foyer with several bullet holes in his chest. Crimson splattered the floor and pooled around the body. The TV was on in the living room.

"What happened?" I asked.

The neighbor across the hall piped up. She was a cute blonde. "My video doorbell captured the whole thing. It goes off every time somebody walks down the hallway. I can't figure out how to shut it off."

She played the footage back on her phone. JD and I huddled around her, watching the display. The scent of her fruity body wash drifted in the air. It mixed with the tinny metallic scent of blood.

A pizza delivery guy knocked on Jesse's door. A motorcycle helmet shielded his face, which wasn't uncommon for these guys. The minute Jesse answered, the delivery guy reached into the insulated red pizza bag and fired two shots through the material.

Jesse's body twitched with each hit, and he fell to the ground, groaning.

The shooter must have used a suppressor to attenuate the sound. But in the enclosed hallway, it was still pretty loud. Loud enough to clip the audio on the doorbell camera.

The delivery guy casually walked away.

A few minutes later, another clip showed the real pizza guy arrive.

It told me that whoever was behind this had put spyware on Jesse's phone, just like we had. It's pretty easy to do remotely. Send a text with a malicious link that will trigger a silent download and install. It allowed them to monitor his call to the pizza joint.

Curious neighbors had discovered the assassination by the time the real delivery guy arrived.

There were no shell casings on the scene. The pizza bag had captured the ejections.

We grabbed surveillance footage of the lobby from the property manager's office. It showed the fake delivery guy entering and exiting. The camera angle caught a view of the parking lot. The assassin climbed on a motorcycle and zipped away, but the license plate of the red sportbike was obscured.

I knew who did this, but proving it would be another story altogether.

Brenda arrived and examined the remains. Jesse's body was bagged, and Paris Delaney was on the scene by the time the corpse was rolled out on a gurney.

"Deputy Wild, is it true the victim was cooperating with prosecutors to uncover a large drug operation?"

"I can't comment at this time," I said.

JD and I left the building and climbed into the Porsche. We headed to the station and filled out after-action reports in the conference room.

Daniels pushed open the door and poked his head in. "Well, I've got a little good news to finish off the day."

JD and I looked at the sheriff with eager eyes.

"I guess someone spread the rumor in the pod that Logan was looking to put a hit on Sydney Voss."

JD shrugged innocently. "I wonder who could have done that."

"Something rattled her cage, and she made a phone call to Logan."

"All phone calls from the jail are recorded," I said, my anticipation growing.

"Want to listen to it?"

I grinned.

The sheriff took a seat at the table, pulled out his cell phone, and played a recording of the clip. It was a low-quality recording, and the line crackled with static.

"What the fuck is going on?" Sydney asked.

"What do you mean?"

"I'm sitting here, keeping my mouth shut while you're out there running around, trying to have me killed."

"What!?"

"Don't play dumb with me!"

"I don't know what you're talking about."

"Bullshit."

"Where are you getting this information from?"

"Newsflash. Word travels fast in here."

"I think you've been misinformed," Logan said.

"Oh, really?"

"Really."

"Why haven't you done anything to get me out of here?"

"I don't have the money. And it would look funny."

"Bullshit, and more bullshit."

"I don't know if you're aware, but my wife kicked me out, and the studio dropped me. I'm a pariah in the industry. All because of my association with you. Excuse me if I need to distance myself in an act of self-preservation."

That was the wrong thing to say.

"Excuse me if I have to implicate a certain someone in a certain crime," Sydney said. "Maybe you *should* hire someone to kill me. Because I'm about to throw you under the bus."

The clip ended, and I asked Daniels, "When was that phone call made?"

"Half an hour ago."

"Has she made any noise about wanting to talk?"

"Not yet."

"Let's get her into an interrogation room and see if we can entice her into a confession," I said.

52

I replayed the audio clip of the conversation for Sydney in the interrogation room.

She didn't seem fazed.

"I think now is the time that you should implicate Logan. You know he's out there trying to make arrangements to shut you up. We have evidence of that."

She lifted a curious brow.

I didn't go into details.

"Hypothetically speaking, if I did implicate him in something, what are you offering?"

"Right now, you're looking at capital murder. That's a life sentence. State's attorney is willing to knock it down to manslaughter. 15 years. *If* your testimony leads to a conviction of your co-conspirator."

She thought about it for a long moment.

I reminded her, "Your fingerprints are on the baggie. Summer saw you enter Tara's stateroom. Your phone call with Logan from the pod is admissible. Not to mention the video from the *Seven Seas* that is floating around on the internet. Maybe it's admissible. Maybe it's not. But it doesn't look good."

Another long moment passed, and her eyes brimmed. "Okay. Let's do this." She cleared her throat. "It was Logan's idea. He gave me the drugs. All I had to do was give them to Tara. She'd put anything up her nose if it was free."

Sydney didn't seem to have any guilt or remorse. She was more upset that she got caught, but she had the satisfaction of knowing she wasn't going down alone.

With her statement, we were able to get a warrant. But in the time it took to coordinate that, Logan had called Kirk. I guess his conversation with Sydney spooked him.

Either way, he was going down. Might as well let him dig his own grave.

Kirk wanted the cash up front, and Logan told him to come by the *Seven Seas*.

JD and I headed over to the posh resort with Kirk, Erickson, and Faulkner.

Paris Delaney and her crew were waiting when we arrived.

I confronted Paris. "What are you doing here?"

"Waiting on a story," she said with a slight smirk.

Through a clenched jaw, I hissed, "This is an undercover operation."

"Don't get your panties in a bunch. I'm not going to ruin anything."

"How did you find out about this? Enough. Tell me who your source is. This is affecting operations."

"Nobody told me anything. We were here already doing a puff piece on the resort. I saw you pull in and figured something was up."

My eyes narrowed at her. I didn't believe it for a second.

She raised her hands innocently. "I swear."

"Stay out of sight," I cautioned.

We followed Kirk down the path that led from the parking lot to the bungalows. We held up at the corner, hiding behind shrubbery as Kirk continued to Logan's bungalow. He was rigged up with a wireless camera again, and we watched on my cell phone.

Kirk knocked on the cabana door, and a moment later, Logan opened.

There was a long moment between the two, then Logan peered outside the bungalow, looking in both directions down the path. He stepped aside, and Kirk stepped into the foyer. Logan closed the door behind them.

"You got the money?" Kirk asked.

Logan nodded.

He escorted Kirk into the living room. There was a duffel bag atop the coffee table. "It's all there. Count it."

Kirk unzipped the black bag and peered inside. There were stacks of hundred-dollar bills. Kirk made sure the camera got a good view.

"The rest upon completion," Kirk said. "If I don't get the rest, I don't need to tell you what happens to you."

"Get the job done, and you'll get your money," Logan said. "But it has to be fast. That bitch has got to stop blabbing."

"When I walk out of that door, this deal is final. There is no going back. Are you sure you want Sydney Voss dead?"

"Yes, and I don't care how you do it as long as that bitch suffers."

"That's all I needed from you."

Kirk grabbed the bag and walked to the front door.

When he pulled it open, we flooded inside with weapons drawn.

I shouted, "Coconut County!"

Erickson and Faulkner had circled around the rear of the bungalow and covered the patio.

Logan's eyes rounded. He froze for a moment, then lurched for the patio, but Erickson and Faulkner put an end to that idea.

With the barrel of my pistol aimed at him, it didn't take much convincing for Logan to raise his hands and surrender.

"On the ground. Face down. Now!"

He complied, and JD slapped the cuffs around his wrists. Logan groaned as the hard steel smacked the bone.

I holstered my pistol once he was secured, then moved to the sliding glass door and pulled it open. Erickson and Faulkner flooded into the room.

We yanked Logan to his feet, and I read him his rights.

Paris Delaney captured the whole thing from the doorway and filmed Logan as we escorted him out of the bungalow and down the path to the parking lot.

He tried to shield his face.

"Why did you try to have Sydney Voss murdered?" Paris asked, knowing the answer.

Logan didn't say anything.

"Are you responsible for the death of Tara DeVille?"

Logan glared at her.

We stuffed him into the back of the patrol car, and he was taken to the station.

Paris stood in front of the camera with the luxury hotel in the background. "Moments ago, Logan Shea was arrested in a bizarre murder for hire plot involving an adult film star and an undercover corrections officer. More on this story as it develops. I'm Paris Delaney, and you heard it from me first."

After Logan had time to sweat in the interrogation room, JD and I entered. I played Kirk's body cam footage of the transaction just to drive home the fact that he was totally screwed.

"Sydney said that you gave her the drugs, and it was your idea to poison Tara."

"She's lying."

"Tell me where you got the drugs from, and maybe there's a little something in it for you."

He scowled at me, not looking very cooperative.

53

"You're going away for the attempted murder of Sydney Voss," I said. "And with her testimony, you're going away for conspiracy to commit murder. I'm guessing you're gonna serve two life sentences."

"With all that, what can you possibly do for me?" Logan asked.

"I don't know if you're aware of this, but there are different ways to do time. A nice minimum-security facility will feel like a luxury resort compared to a maximum-security penitentiary filled with murderers and rapists, all of whom would love to get a piece of you."

The color drained from his face, and his skin misted with sweat.

"I just want a name," I said. "I want to get that stuff off the streets, even if it was a special concoction you crafted."

He was silent for a moment. His nervous eyes darted about, and his mind reeled. "I never conspired to kill anybody," he said.

I didn't buy it for a second.

"It was just talk. I didn't think anything of it. I sure as hell didn't think she'd actually do it."

I gave him an incredulous look.

"All I said was *I hope that bitch ODs. It wouldn't be hard to slip her something.*" That was it. That's all I said."

"So, how did Sydney get the drugs?"

He shrugged innocently. "Look, I keep a little coke on hand. Everybody does. Nothing wrong with that. You drink coffee. I perk up with a little nose candy."

"Not quite the same, is it?"

"We all have our own vices."

"What about the fentanyl?"

"I keep a little around for pain."

"Pain?"

"I've got a torn rotator cuff. Sometimes I tweak it when I hit the gym."

Jack and I exchanged a glance. JD could certainly relate to shoulder problems.

"So you're telling me that Sydney, on her own, stole your stash, mixed together a lethal cocktail, and gave it to Tara?"

"That's exactly what I'm saying. She saw that movie. That's probably where she got the idea."

"Tell me who your supplier is?"

He hesitated a moment. "Just this guy I met at a club. Miguel."

JD and I exchanged a knowing glance. All roads were leading back to Hugo Ortega. But with Logan's public arrest, there was no way we could set up a sting with Miguel. And we had nothing on the big guy. As usual, Hugo Ortega would remain unscathed.

We left the station and headed to *Diver Down*. We took a seat at the bar, and Teagan poured us drinks.

We took a moment to celebrate. It might not have been nice and neat, but we managed to get most of the players behind bars. They would all do time. Maybe not the maximum, but something was better than nothing.

JD lifted his glass to toast. We clinked and sipped the fine whiskey.

Paris Delaney appeared on the flatscreen behind the bar, replaying the arrest of Logan.

My phone buzzed with a call from Jacko, the manager at *Forbidden Fruit*. "I think I found your missing girl."

"Evangeline?"

"Yep. She's alive and well and just showed up to work."

I lifted a surprised brow. "Where has she been for the last few weeks?"

"Went to Europe with a client. Some last-minute deal after she got back from her ride on the submarine. Lost her phone. You can call off the dogs."

"That's a relief. Has she talked to her brother?"

"Hey, I just work here."

"Thanks for the heads up."

"Anytime."

I ended the call and updated JD.

"Maybe we need to make a trip to *Forbidden Fruit* just to make sure she's not an imposter."

I laughed.

"Now that these cases are pretty much wrapped up, you know what we need to do?"

I knew exactly where he was going.

"We need to get out there and look for the HMS Silverstone."

"The Silverstone?" Teagan asked, perking up.

Jack leaned in and whispered. "Can you keep a secret?"

54

My phone buzzed the nightstand around 4 AM the next morning. Calls from the sheriff at this hour were never good. My dry, scratchy voice could barely sound the words. "What is it?"

"You need to get over to the *Platinum Dunes Estates*. 1313 Shore Breeze Drive."

The address sounded familiar, but at this hour of the morning, I wasn't firing on all cylinders. It took a moment. "That's Hugo Ortega's place."

"Was."

"Was?"

"Somebody took him out with a high-powered rifle."

That hung there for a moment.

"As far as I'm concerned, someone did the world a favor. But get over there and check it out."

I ended the call, pulled myself out of bed, and got dressed. I press-checked my weapon and holstered it for an appendix carry, then rousted JD out of bed.

We headed over to the posh estates. Emergency lighting flickered from an ambulance in front of the house. Two patrol cars were on the scene, lights flashing.

JD parked the Spyder at the curb. We hopped out and followed the trail of responders up the driveway to the patio near the pool.

Hugo Ortega, and his right-hand man Miguel, lay on the ground, poolside. Both had taken a shot to the chest. Blood splattered their suits and pooled around their bodies. Hugo had stepped onto the patio with a drink in his hand. That drink was now shattered into pieces at his side.

Brenda hovered over the remains, wearing pink nitrile gloves.

"Time of death?" I asked.

"Hour ago, give or take," she said.

I surveyed the area. There was a nice pool, glowing with underwater lighting. Tall spires of evergreens lined the pool. Beyond was a canal with an 82-foot SunTrekker yacht. Across the canal were more luxury mansions. Lights from houses across the water glowed.

"You think somebody came in via the canal and shot him from the dock?" JD asked.

"Could be," I said.

We walked across the lawn to the canal and looked around. It was less than 50 yards from the back door.

I didn't see any shell casings on the dock.

I looked across the canal to the home directly behind Hugo's. There were no lights on in the house, but the terrace door was slightly ajar.

We walked back up the lawn and rejoined the others.

"Neighbors see or hear anything?" I asked.

Deputy Thacker shook his head. "I talked to the neighbors on either side. Nothing."

I nodded to JD, and we hustled down the driveway, hopped into the Porsche and twisted through the streets, finding the house directly across the canal from Hugo's. There was a for sale sign in the yard, and I figured the house was vacant.

We hustled up the walkway to the front door and rang the bell. Nobody answered. I peered through the windows.

There was no furniture in the house.

I tried the front door, but it was locked.

JD and I moved around the side of the house to the back-yard. A glass pane had been broken out of the back window. Someone had reached their hand inside and unlatched the deadbolt.

I drew my pistol, twisted the handle, and pushed open the door. I didn't expect anyone to be there, but better safe than sorry.

Shards of glass sparkled on the floor in the moonlight.

We stepped inside, and bits of glass crunched under my feet.

The alarm wasn't on. I figured the realtor who last showed the house had forgotten to set it.

I used a tactical flashlight to illuminate the way. The beam swept through the house as I crept through the kitchen, across the living room, and up the central staircase. We took the long hallway to the master bedroom, clearing each room as we passed. We were careful to avoid stepping on the footprints on the plush carpet.

I pushed open the door to the master bedroom and swept my barrel across the room. The beam of my flashlight pierced the darkness and illuminated the empty room.

It was clear.

Impressions in the carpet led from the terrace to the entry door. They could have been anybody's footprints. Anybody with small feet. They could have been old or new. It was hard to say when the last time the carpet was vacuumed.

We crossed the bedroom and checked the closet and bathroom.

All clear.

The french doors to the terrace were unlocked and slightly ajar.

JD and I stepped outside.

The terrace was spacious, with a few lounge chairs and a wet bar. A concrete balustrade secured the perimeter.

The terrace offered a perfect vantage point. A clear shot across the canal to Hugo's patio. At a little over 100 yards, it would've been an easy shot for a professional. With a suppressor, the noise might not have woken up neighbors at this hour. Two quick shots and the shooter was gone.

I looked around the terrace for shell casings but didn't see anything. This was a professional hit. There was no doubt in my mind. I surveyed the area where I would set up for a shot.

Snagged on the concrete baluster was a single strand of long brunette hair.

I took a deep breath. My chest tightened. I had a feeling I knew exactly who the shooter was.

A gust of wind carried the strand away before I could collect it.

I can't say that the demise of Hugo Ortega was upsetting. But this was one case that I didn't want to pursue to conclusion, afraid of where it might lead.

Ready for more?

The adventure continues with Wild Fire!

Join my newsletter and find out what happens next!

AUTHOR'S NOTE

Thanks for all the great reviews!

I've got more adventures for Tyson and JD. Stay tuned.

If you liked this book, let me know with a review on Amazon.

Thanks for reading!

—*Tripp*

TYSON WILD

Wild Ocean

Wild Justice

Wild Rivera

Wild Tide

Wild Rain

Wild Captive

Wild Killer

Wild Honor

Wild Gold

Wild Case

Wild Crown

Wild Break

Wild Fury

Wild Surge

Wild Impact

Wild L.A.

Wild High

Wild Abyss

Wild Life

Wild Spirit

Wild Thunder

Wild Season

Wild Rage

Wild Heart

Wild Spring

Wild Outlaw

Wild Revenge

Wild Secret

Wild Envy

Wild Surf

Wild Venom

Wild Island

Wild Demon

Wild Blue

Wild Lights

Wild Target

Wild Jewel

Wild Greed

Wild Sky

Wild Storm

Wild Bay

Wild Chaos

Wild Cruise

Wild Catch

Wild Encounter

Wild Blood

Wild Vice

Wild Winter

Wild Malice

Wild Fire

Wild...

CONNECT WITH ME

I'm just a geek who loves to write. Follow me on Facebook.

www.trippellis.com

Made in United States
North Haven, CT
18 September 2023

41697764R00178